RIVAL

Rival

SARA BENNETT WEALER

HARPER TEEN

An Imprint of HarperCollinsPublishers

HarperTeen is an imprint of HarperCollins Publishers.

Rival

Copyright © 2011 by Sara Bennett Wealer

Library of Congress Cataloging-in-Publication Data
Bennett Wealer, Sara.
    Rival / Sara Bennett Wealer. — 1st ed.
       p.   cm.
    Summary: Two high school rivals compete in a prestigious singing competition while reflecting on the events that turned them from close friends to enemies the year before.
    ISBN 978-0-06-182762-4
    [1. Singing—Fiction. 2. Contests—Fiction. 3. Friendship—Fiction. 4. Popularity—Fiction. 5. High schools—Fiction. 6. Schools—Fiction. 7. Interpersonal relations—Fiction.] I. Title.
PZ7.B447111Ri 2011   2010003092
[Fic]—dc22   CIP
                                                AC

Typography by Torborg Davern
11 12 13 14 15 LP/RRDB 10 9 8 7 6 5 4 3 2
❖
First Edition

FOR MY DAUGHTERS

SENIOR YEAR

*Dissonance: a harsh sounding of notes that produces a
feeling of tension and unrest*

KATHRYN

I SAW AN OLD COMMERCIAL once where famous singers used their voices to shatter glass. So I looked into it last year for a project in physics class, and it didn't take much of a Google search to find out the whole thing is pretty much a myth. Theoretically, the sound waves created by vibrating vocal cords could break a crystal goblet if they resonated long enough at just the right pitch, but finding and holding a note like that is incredibly difficult. The human voice, it turns out, just isn't that strong.

Human hatred, on the other hand, is. Anybody who doubts that should stand where I am right now and feel the hate waves coming off of Brooke Dempsey.

We're halfway through the second day of senior year, and both of us are in the back row of the Honors Choir; me in the soprano section, Brooke nine spots over with the altos. Even with all those people between us, even with our folders up, our eyes on Mr. Anderson, and our voices busy on a really hard Bach cantata, I feel a steady *ping* coming off of Brooke like the signal from a giant antenna. It's like this every time we're in the same room—she's tracking me, I'm tracking her. The Defense Department would kill to have radar this good.

"Watch it, people!" Mr. Anderson shouts as the tempo picks up, the beats get more complex, and people start hunching over their music as if that will make the notes easier to sing. For a few measures I can hear Brooke's deep voice above everybody else's. I start using my pencil to beat time against my folder and she homes in even tighter. The waves coming from her direction are like a battering ram; I swear I can feel them against the entire length of my body. But I don't shatter; I'm not made of glass. Anyway, the parts that break aren't on the outside.

"Stop, stop, stop!" Mr. Anderson shouts, flapping his arms. The Bach has gotten the best of us and people start to look worried, because those of us who have been in the choir for a few years know what's coming next. "I asked you to study the repertoire over the summer, folks," he says. "Give me a quintet. Down front, now. Steve Edwards, baritone. Tenor, Matt McWalter. Brooke, you're our alto." Once I hear Brooke's name I know mine will be called, too. Mr. Anderson only calls people for quintets if he thinks they're slacking or if they're really,

really good. Brooke and I get called when he wants to demonstrate how a piece *should* be done; we get called because we're the two best singers at our school.

"Great," comes a voice from behind, and I turn to see Matt, my best friend, trudging down the risers after me. I smile apologetically, but secretly I'm glad he's in the quintet, too. Matt isn't just my best friend, he's pretty much my only friend—the one person to stick by me after Brooke started this cold war by punching me in front of half the student body after last year's Homecoming dance.

For a minute, while everybody gets situated, she and I almost brush up against each other; the nearness of her makes my skin tingle as my nose fills with her green tea and chlorine scent. Laura Lindner, a second soprano, steps between us as we line up bass, tenor, alto, SII, and SI, but I can still see Brooke out of the corner of my eye— that regal profile with the nose just this side of too big, the sun-streaked hair, the icy blue eyes. Brooke is beautiful in a way that's hard to describe, like the perfect parts of other people have been reassembled, slightly imperfectly, into a girl who looks like she'd be just as at home in a Greek forum as she is in the hallways of William O. Douglas High School. She towers over the rest of us while we get our music ready.

"Folders up!" Mr. Anderson commands. The pianist

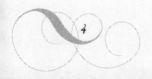

plays the introduction, we launch into the piece, and then something rare happens: Just for a moment, I forget about Brooke. The music is beautiful and challenging and fun to sing. I stare at the back wall, past Mr. Anderson's conducting arm, allowing the notes to spool from memory out of my throat.

"Nice, nice . . . ," he tells the group when we're finished. "But most of you have too much vibrato. Try singing it like Kathryn just did, with a nice, straight tone."

Pleased with the compliment and still lost in the music, I turn to smile at Matt, but I catch Brooke's eye instead. She grimaces as if to say, *You've* got *to be kidding me*, then snickers and elbows Laura, who laughs, too. Nobody else notices, and I know from experience that pointing it out—getting upset—would only make me look bad. After that humiliating Homecoming punch, I looked into my bathroom mirror to find a purpling welt across my left cheekbone. These days when Brooke strikes, there's nothing to show where the blow landed; she's become an expert at leaving no marks.

I guess you could say that Brooke Dempsey and I are rivals. That's not entirely accurate, though, because if you look it up in the dictionary "rival" means "one that equals or almost equals another." If anything, Brooke and I are complete opposites. Her voice is deep and rich, mine is high and airy. She's imposing and confident, I'm small and . . . not. Socially we're on different planets altogether, the biggest difference being that Brooke is ridiculously popular.

Why, then, should somebody like her care enough to hate somebody like me?

It's a long story.

BROOKE

I DON'T LIKE KATHRYN PEASE. That doesn't make me evil or anything. I'm just not one of those people who thinks everybody has to go around being nice to everybody else all the time. I could pretend everything's fine between us. I could be nice to her face, then trash her behind her back. But I think it's better to be honest. I don't like Kathryn, and I'm not afraid to admit it.

Unfortunately for her, if I don't like somebody you can bet nobody else does, either. My best friend Chloe says it's a power thing—people pay attention to who's on my bad side because they don't want to end up there, too. But I think that's only part of it. Kathryn does a pretty good job turning people off all by herself.

Take right now, for example. We're down front in Honors Choir. In one of Anderson's quintets, which are really no big deal. But from the way Kathryn's going after it you would think this was the Met. She's singing way too loud.

Even has the music memorized. When we're done, Anderson starts gushing about her "nice, straight tone," and she looks over at me—right at me—with this bitchy little smile on her face.

"Ow!" whispers Laura Lindner when I elbow her in the arm. "What's the deal?"

"I'd have a nice, straight tone, too," I whisper, "if I had a nice, straight stick up my ass."

Laura laughs. Kathryn looks away. And she doesn't look at me again for the rest of the rehearsal. Choir would be my favorite class if it wasn't for her.

I know. Choir. It sounds lame. And if you were Chloe, that's exactly what you'd say. *You can do whatever you want, Brooke. You're a Dempsey! So how come you're wasting your time with the music freaks?*

But she has no idea. None of the people we hang out with have any idea how big a deal music really is at our school. You'd think they would have gotten a hint when the Honors Choir performed at the White House—not one of those trips where you get to go if you sell enough popcorn, but a real concert set up by the First Lady and broadcast on public television. Or when two years in a row, somebody from William O. Douglas won the Blackmore Young Artists' Festival, which is one of the biggest voice competitions in the country and just happens to take place at Baldwin University, right up the road. But it doesn't have anything to do with sports or getting wasted or hooking up, so music might as well be knitting or ballroom dancing as far as they're concerned.

Music, however, is my life.

It's also the one place where I can't get rid of Kathryn.

She and I have other things that we're good at, of course. I swim. She writes for the school newspaper. But music is our main focus. Some days the only thing that keeps us from ripping each other apart is the fact that we're different voice types, which means we don't usually go up for the same parts.

We've always known, though, that that was going to change.

The bell rings, and while we're putting away our folders Anderson picks up two yellow envelopes from the podium.

"People!" he shouts. "Don't forget the pool party at Brooke's after school. One last hurrah before we start the contest season! And speaking of contests—Brooke, can I see you for a moment? Kathryn, you too."

We both head down to the front of the room, but Kathryn hangs back a little. It's like she thinks I'll bite or something.

"You've been waiting for these, I believe?" says Anderson as he gives one envelope to me, the other one to her.

She thanks him. Puts the envelope into her bag, and

hurries out of the room. I see her take it out when she's halfway down the hall. She opens it and reads while she walks, her dark ponytail swinging.

I wait until I get home to open mine.

Congratulations. You have been selected to participate in the 50th Anniversary Blackmore Young Artists' Festival.

I sit on my bed and open the pamphlet that came with the letter. I read the section about the contest history—how Ian Buxton Blackmore came to Lake Champion after a highly successful opera career and started the contest to get our singers into the elite music world. I scan the list of past winners—they end up at Juilliard, at Peabody, in Europe singing with major orchestras. I imagine my own name on that list. This is what I've been working for ever since we moved to Minnesota.

And it's going to be my ticket out of here.

Finally, I flip to the contest rules, even though I've been to every Blackmore for the past seven years and I know everything by heart. There's only one first prize in the vocal division, so different voice types don't matter. It's sopranos against tenors. Baritones against altos. Altos against sopranos. Me against Kathryn.

The letter has a link to an online registration form. I grab my laptop and fill it out, listing all the voice teachers I've had. Especially the ones in New York, which is a big deal since not many singers from here can afford

training like that. Just to be safe, I rip out the snail mail entry and fill that out, too. Then I walk to the post office and send it priority with delivery tracking. This way, I know that the entry is on its way—that *I* am on *my* way. For the past two years, somebody from our school has won the Blackmore. This year is my turn. All I have to do is keep Kathryn in her place, which should be easy when you consider who I am, and who she is.

But I learned a long time ago that you can't assume anything when it comes to her.

I learned it the hard way.

KATHRYN

"A WHOLE HALF HOUR YOU'VE been out in the sun and it hasn't burned a hole in you yet. Guess the rumors aren't true."

Matt lies back in a lawn chair, folds his arms behind his head, and sighs contentedly. We've claimed a spot near the fence that separates Brooke's yard from her neighbors', a perfect place for watching the pool party while remaining fairly inconspicuous. From here, it looks like one of the movies Matt and I rent every Saturday night. Pretty girls lounge alongside the pool, paying just enough attention to the guys in the water to let the guys know it's worth the effort of showing off, while the less attractive people huddle around the food table. Meanwhile, the serious sun worshippers are using this opportunity to catch the last of the day's rays.

But while Matt's basking, I'm stewing. The word "rumor" has set off a loop in my brain—a buzzing blip that repeats, over and over: *Brooke. What is she saying about me now?*

"What rumors?" I say.

"That you're a vampire. Everybody's talking about it." The joke is only partly funny, and he seems to sense that because he follows up with, "Well, not everybody. Just me, myself, and I. We'd do anything to get your nose out of those books."

He looks pointedly at my hands, which clutch a dog-eared copy of *Waiting for Godot*. I look down and realize I've been rolling the pages back as I read them; the cover is streaked with creases and will probably never lie flat again.

"I know. This is a study-free zone." I close the book and roll it even tighter. "But I already have a paper due in AP English. And Sunday I'm singing for that scholarship committee from Cincinnati, which is a long shot because they don't have a lot of money this year, but my mom set it up, which means I have to do it, and that means I'm going to lose prep time for Human Anatomy. . . ."

"Whoa there, Glaurung!" Matt thrusts out his arms, making a cross like a knight warding off a dragon. "Now you're stressing *me* out."

"Ugh," I moan. "I'm sorry." I unroll the book, stash it under my thigh, and try to push aside the feeling that

I should be doing something productive all of the time.

"See? I knew you needed a break." He sits up and reaches around to pat himself on the back. "Good on me for forcing you out today. Ow!"

Wincing, he pulls back his T-shirt to reveal a burn blooming along his neckline. I laugh. "Who's the vampire now? Without me to drag around, you'd be holed up in World of Warfare."

"So we're both pathetic." He drapes a towel gingerly over his shoulders. "I vote we change that. Come with me to the pool?"

I freeze. Just coming to the party was a big step. I haven't seen Brooke yet, but I can just imagine her finding and following me with that superstrong radar.

"I'm fine right here," I say. "Thanks."

Another pointed look. After ten years, I can almost read Matt's mind. The trouble is that he can read mine, too, and whereas I've had to learn my skill, he's had his from the start—ever since the first day of second-grade Sunday school, when he came to where I'd huddled into a corner, sat down next to me, and didn't say a word. He biked over to our house the next afternoon, and though I told my mom I didn't want to play, secretly I was glad somebody wanted to be my friend. We rode our bikes up and down the sidewalk, Matt chattering question after question whether I answered or not. He would just pretend that I had, and most of the time his pretend answers were exactly what I would have said anyway.

Eventually I started to open up and we've been best friends ever since. I helped him keep up his grades when ADHD combined with a raging sci-fi and fantasy obsession put him in the principal's office more hours than he ever spent in class, and he helped me bear the infinitely awkward contradiction of being an overachiever who loathes the spotlight. One Sunday, the teacher taught us the song about letting your little light shine. Everybody loved the part where you sing "hide it under a bushel," and then shout "NO!" Especially Matt, who would get right in my face and scream "NO!" as loud as he could. After that, whenever he caught me being reclusive he would sing the bushel song. It was his way of pulling me out, telling me not to take myself too seriously.

These days he just gets right to the point.

"You've got to get over this thing with Brooke, Kath. It's been a year."

"But it's Brooke." I study his face, trying to read whether he senses something about her that I've missed. Matt is a scarily accurate judge of character, especially after years of refereeing online fandoms and meeting total strangers at sci-fi conventions. "You remember how bad it got."

He smiles. Those comforting brown eyes crinkle at the edges, one of them nearly hidden under a flop of long hair.

"Time has passed and people change," he says. "We'll all be going to college anyway. I seriously doubt she's still thinking about what happened last year."

I want to believe he's right, but I'm not so sure. I don't feel like *I've* changed all that much.

"Obviously you weren't watching in choir today," I say. "And then there's this." I pull my book out and hold up the yellow envelope I've been using to mark my place. Peeking out of the frayed opening is a pamphlet I've read three times now, six if you count all of the times I went over the section on prize money. A twenty-five-thousand-dollar check for first place; my jaw clenches when I think about my parents and how worried they've been about my college savings.

"You made it to the Blackmore?" He leans over and wraps a sunburned arm around my shoulder. "That's awesome! Why didn't you tell me?"

"I didn't tell anybody."

"Not even your mom and dad? They're going to freak."

"Exactly." I put the envelope back into the book. "Once they know I'm in, they're going to put all their hopes on it. The prize money is more than any of the scholarships I've applied for. Plus, it's one hundred and fifty dollars just for the entry. I don't have that kind of money."

"You can scrape up fifty bucks, right?"

"Yes . . ."

"Then I'll tell my parents it's an emergency and we'll put the rest on my credit card. Now, what's your real reason?"

"Well . . ." I hesitate. Lately I've harbored this fantasy of not competing—of finding the money I need someplace else and avoiding what is bound to turn into a musical showdown between Brooke and me.

"So we're back to *her* again," says Matt. He squeezes my shoulder and then stands. "I really think you'd be surprised, Kath. Brooke probably doesn't even care anymore."

He holds out his hand, yet I can't seem to get up. I lower my eyes, tilt my head, and let the right corner of my mouth creep into a half smile. We call this the Matt Melter™, and it can be used for many purposes, such as convincing him to let me have the last of the onion soup dip during our weekend movie nights. Usually I only use the Matt Melter™ for good, but today calls for desperate measures.

"Studious cat iz studious," I say. "I can haz hall pass?"

"Don't try to lolspeak your way out of this one," he laughs. "And turn off the Matt Melter. It won't work, either."

"You forgot the tee em," I pout.

"And you forgot about my superatomic powers of persuasion. Seriously. I'll sic my *Doctor Who* fanboys on you, and you'll never be able to go online again."

For my birthday last year, Matt gave my email address and IM to his Tolkien message board, and for weeks my in-box was clogged with birthday greetings in Elvish and Numenorian. But beyond my fear of spamming space opera fans is the recognition that Matt is right: We've been loners for too long.

Maybe he's right about Brooke, too; maybe this entire rivalry is all in my head, kept alive because I've been afraid to move on. After all the time that's passed, maybe it's time we did.

I let him lead me to the side of the pool and we sit, dangling our feet in the water.

"Nice?" says Matt.

I adjust the straps of my tank top and have to admit that it *is* nice. The heat is beginning to break, and the breeze has just a hint of chill in it. Locusts are whirring in the big old trees. The sun has started to set, giving the sky an orange and lavender petticoat—

Splash!

Water sloshes into my lap, and I look down to see a Marvin the Martian tattoo disappear under the waves beneath my feet. Marvin is attached to Tim McNamara, the only other A-lister in Honors, besides Brooke. Tim probably would never have even thought about choir if Mr. Anderson hadn't heard about his super-humanly deep baritone and begged him to join.

He comes up and aims another splash in my direction. I try to sound light as I hold up my hands to catch the spray.

"Quit it!" I laugh.

"You're too dry," Tim says. "Got to fix that."

"I'm fine. Really. I don't want to get wet."

"Which is exactly why you need to."

He grabs my ankles and panic shoots through me. I feel him tug, feel the concrete pool deck scrape my thighs, see the water lurch closer as my wet shorts start to slide on the drain tiles.

"No!" I shout, wrenching out of his grasp and scooting away from the edge. I pull my knees to my chest so he can't grab me again.

"Hey, man," Matt says before Tim can process what just happened. "You know who'd really be fun to haul in there? Leslie Sauer. She's been hanging out by the stairs trying to pretend like that swimsuit isn't see-through."

Tim looks over at Leslie, who adjusts and readjusts a sarong over her butter yellow one-piece, then he gives a wicked laugh and swims off in her direction. I hear a splash, hear her scream, and feel bad that my rescue has to come at her expense.

"Kathryn?" Matt says. "You okay?"

"Yes." I untangle my legs from my arms. "I'm sorry. I'm an idiot."

He puts his hands on my knees, gently pushing so that my toes touch the pool deck. "You're not an idiot." He pats the spot next to him and I scoot forward. "Want to wait here for a second?" he asks. "I'm going to get a soda."

I nod and he stands, heading for the cooler by the kitchen door. When he passes the gazebo, one of the basses calls out and pulls him into their group. Matt may be a loner, but most of the time it's by choice. I've always sort of admired the way he can fit in when he wants to.

The gazebo basses point out a tenor in a Speedo who's doing swan dives off the diving board. Matt laughs and the other guys laugh, and when I look around it seems as if everybody is laughing. They're hopping in and out of the water like penguins, cheering one another on as they leap off the diving board, splashing the surface and cutting through the deep water like it's the easiest thing in the world.

Meanwhile, I am sitting here alone—probably the only seventeen-year-old anywhere who still doesn't know how to swim.

BROOKE

"SO I TOLD JACK HE could do the shareholders meeting without me. I need a break, and I'm taking one." Mom is standing at the kitchen sink, cutting cantaloupe into a big melon bowl. She looks out the window and lets out a deep breath. "God, it's nice to get away from those tightasses on the board. Young people are so refreshing."

I want to retch. She's got her back to me, so she doesn't see me making a face while I pile soda cans into a bucketful of ice. Mom gets like this whenever I have people over. She likes to pretend she's part of the group, not the PR director for the biggest bank in town. Today she took off her business suit and put on hot pants, a Hawaiian shirt, and kitten heels with fake fur on the toes that I remember from back when she used to sing cabaret. Considering what she usually wears when my friends are here, this is pretty tame. But that doesn't mean I trust her. Even though people are showing up left and right, I'm stuck in the kitchen making sure she and my twin brothers don't soak the watermelon in vodka. This isn't like the parties they're used to, where kids run around getting wasted and doing whatever they want. The crowd today is totally different.

"Okay, I'm lost." The screen door slides open and Bill Jr. flip-flops in wearing a tank top with his fraternity letters on it. He goes to the fridge and takes out a bottle of beer. "Call me senile, but I don't recognize anybody. Who are these people again?"

"They're from Honors Choir," I say.

"I remember some of them," comes a voice from the breakfast nook. Brice has been holed up in there playing computer games since lunch. He was the school mascot his senior year, which means he got to dress up like a pirate and travel with the marching band. He and Bill go to the University of Minnesota now.

Brice comes out with an empty scotch glass in his hand. He refills it. Then he goes to the fridge and starts pulling out packages of hamburger and hot dogs. Mom does a little dance to the music coming in through the window while she adds grapes to the fruit salad.

"Where's Chloe?" Brice asks me. "I thought you two were inseparable."

"Chloe's not here," I say. Out on the patio, I see Isabelle Jovet pick up my iPod and start surfing. "His Name

Is Lancelot" starts to blare over the speakers. "This isn't exactly her crowd."

"It's not exactly your crowd, either," says Bill Jr.

"It's totally my crowd."

"Oh yes. Brookehilde is a serious musician!" Brice balances his scotch on top of the meat while he reaches for a pair of tongs. "Take care, O plebes, lest ye drag her down into the uncultured masses."

I shoot him a look. "I'm just saying. Not every party has to be about getting wasted. I have other friends, you know."

"And they're nice kids," says Mom. "It's wonderful Brooke is so popular."

"A miracle, too," Brice adds as he heads out the back door. "Considering she's so cranky all the time."

"Hello!" I shout, lunging for his drink. "Did you not hear me? Not that kind of party. My choir teacher is here. Do you want to get me kicked out?"

Mom stops dancing and puts on her serious face. "Yes, good point. This is a school-sanctioned activity. Let's be on our best behavior, okay?"

Brice and Bill bitch about having to stay sober. I figured they would. But after a few minutes, when it's obvious I'm not giving in, they go outside and leave Mom and me alone in the kitchen. I need to get to the party, but there's something I've been wanting to talk to her about. She's in a good mood. I figure now's as good a time as any.

"I made it into the Blackmore," I tell her.

"You did? That's fantastic." No congratulations. No hug. She cuts up a strawberry, arranges it in a fan shape on top of her fruit salad, then sucks the juice off her fingers.

"So I think I'm going to New York in the next week or so. I want to see if Dad can set me up with some coaching."

As soon as I mention him, her face gets all pinched.

"You have coaching here," she tells me.

"Those are just my regular lessons. I need a more professional opinion."

"I don't think it's a good idea."

"Why?"

"You have school."

"I can miss a few days. All I'm taking is electives."

Mom puts down her knife. "I said I don't think it's a good idea. If your father wants to bring himself here that's one thing, but I'm not allowing you to interrupt your last year of high school just so you can chase him all over New York City. Besides, who knows if he'll even be in New York? He might be on a new project. Or Jake could be on location somewhere."

"I'll stay in their apartment, then. I've done it before."

"No."

She looks ridiculous in her loud shirt and fuzzy shoes, talking to me like I'm twelve. She can talk all she wants about the tightasses at her office, but the truth is, when it comes to me and singing, she's the biggest tightass of all. A long time ago she was daring. Back when she sang, when we lived in Manhattan and Dad was working as a Broadway set designer. But then Dad met Jake and everything changed.

Jake Jaspers is a movie star. So huge that nobody's supposed to talk about him and Dad being together—not even me or Mom or the twins. When Dad met him Jake was a semifamous stage actor who was just starting to get some Hollywood interest. I guess it was love at first sight because within three months Dad was moving out of our apartment. Mom freaked. She really had no idea he was gay. And all of a sudden she got obsessed with security. She decided she'd never be able to raise the twins and me on what she made as a singer, so when a friend in the Financial District told her one of their bank branches needed somebody in PR, she packed us up for Minnesota as soon as the offer was official.

I was eleven then. Now I'm almost eighteen. And next year I *will* be going back. The last girl from our school who won the Blackmore got a part in a new Broadway musical. The girl who won two years ago went straight to Juilliard.

"This contest is ten times more important than school," I tell Mom.

"Brooke." She gives me her "responsible parent" look. "I understand—"

"Good," I interrupt. "Then I won't have to go behind your back or anything." I reach past her for the watermelon boat. Then I bump open the back door and step out onto the patio.

Almost immediately, I feel better. I've got show tunes on the stereo. Fruit salad, which does look tasty even if my mom made it. Plus the entire Honors Choir hanging out in my backyard. There aren't any cheerleaders prancing around refusing to get their hair wet. There isn't a keg in the corner, so there aren't any drunks making fools out of themselves. The tenors are sunning on the deck chairs like they're in Saint-Tropez. A few feet away some girls are popping up and down in the shallow end, trying to sing our new Palestrina chorale underwater. When I walk through the crowd, nobody tries to pull me into some "she said/she said" drama. The choir people are cool, which is what I've always loved about them. They seem happy to just be themselves.

"Hey, Brooke," they say. "Hey."

I can tell from their voices and the way they step back as I go by that they think it's a big deal to be at my house. Which makes me feel crappy that I haven't done a party like this sooner.

"There you are, Brooke." Anderson takes my elbow and leads me over to the diving board. "I was just getting ready to do the welcome. Any chance of turning down Tim Curry?"

"Sure!" I run over to the stereo and put *Spamalot* on pause. He gets everybody's attention and then launches into the speech he gives every year, pumping us up for the hard work ahead.

"Special thanks, of course, go to Brooke for hosting tonight," he says, motioning me over. I stand next to him looking out over the pool. Everybody applauds, and it gets to me again—they're acting like it's an honor to hang out here when the truth is that, if I had to choose between these guys and my other friends, I'd probably pick the singers any day.

Anderson turns to me. "You're a senior, Brooke. Anything you want to say?"

I'm totally not big on sappy speeches. I'd rather do something fun. Over everybody's heads I catch Bill Jr. looking at me, and I can hear his voice from back in the kitchen: *This isn't exactly your crowd.*

Like hell it isn't.

"Um . . . well, first off thanks for coming. I'm totally proud of everything we've done together so far, and I know this is going to be the best year yet." As I talk, I start nudging Anderson. Nudge, nudge, nudge . . . until he has to step away so I can get onto the diving board. "For all you new people, here's a warning. Anderson is going to make us do a bunch of really hard stuff. You know, serious. So I say we at least start off the season with something fun. Right? Okay! Folders up!"

People start giggling. I give the first two notes: *"Once more . . ."* And they know exactly where I'm going: *" . . . Gondolieri both skillful and wary, free from this quandary contented are we!"*

Right away, no matter where they are, people fall into their parts, swaying in time. It's *The Gondoliers*, our finale number from State last year—the one where we got the highest score of any ensemble in the history of the contest. It's a fast song and it's cheesy and it's impossible not to have a blast singing it.

It's also totally cool. Where else can people just start singing opera and have it sound awesome?

The end is coming. I grab a water noodle for a baton and give the signal for people to slow down and get quiet. *"Once more . . ."*

They start the build: *"Ga-haaaaaan-dooooooooh-lieri, Gondolieri, Gondolieri contented are we!"*

The sopranos in the shallow end are bobbing up and down. *"Ah-ah, ah-ah!"*

The tenors on the lawn chairs start waving their towels. *"Ah-ah, ah-ah!"*

And then we all go, superfast, to the last, superhigh note at the end.

Old Xeres adieu Manzanilla Montero
We'll leave you with feelings of pleasure with feeli...
*   of plea-heeeeeeeeh-sure!*

Everybody whoops and cheers. Over the fence, the Madigans, who are having a family grillout, start to clap, too. I rip off my T-shirt so I'm in my swimsuit. Then I charge down the diving board. Anderson covers his head like he's afraid I'll pull him in with me. I run past him and do a cannonball, right into the middle of the deep end.

By the time I dry off, the party has kicked into high gear. A bunch of people are hanging out under the gazebo, so I head over there, too. On the way, I pass Bill at the grill. I smile a smile that says, *See? Totally my crowd* just as Brice comes over with a plate full of corn on the cob.

"So is that one guy coming?" he asks me. "Newish guy. I talked to him when those football players were over the other day. John Something-house. Where's he at?"

I get a chill, and it's not just from being wet. John Moorehouse is probably the hottest guy at school. He moved here from Iowa in the spring, and it didn't take him long to get established. Now he's a big deal on the football team. He's also a big deal to me.

"It's not that kind of party," I remind Brice, although

...e where I wish it was. If I could
...just one thing from my other life
...Moorehouse would definitely be it.
...s. "He was telling me how to crack
...Squirrels 2, but I forgot which nuts
...teeth of perpetual immunity."

...to discuss the finer points of their video game and grab a chair under the gazebo. Beach balls haven't been blown up yet, so I grab a package just as Laura Lindner plops down next to me.

"Your brothers are adorable," she says. "It's so cool they came back for your party, Brooke."

Her mousy hair is in a too-tight ponytail, and she's wearing surf jams that might have been in style two years ago but are totally out now. I guess she's decided we're best friends, since I talked to her in that quintet this afternoon.

"College hasn't actually started," I tell her. "They go back on Sunday."

"Well, it's still cool they're *here*. I mean, it's like they still know everybody."

I look over at the twins, who are trying to socialize and run the grill at the same time. They really are good actors. Every person who goes up to them is like some long-lost friend they're ecstatic to see.

On the table, my cell phone starts ringing. I lean over,

check the caller ID, and then go back to my beach ball.

"Don't you need to get that?" Laura says.

"It's just Chloe."

"Oh!" Laura pushes the phone toward me. "You should totally take it." She turns her chair around to let me talk in private.

"So how's the freak show?" Chloe asks.

I pretend I didn't hear her. "You're breaking up. Where are you?" I can hear music and crowd noise in the background.

"Pomodori's!" she shouts. "Spirit Committee meeting! I told them to pick someplace else 'cause the pizza here sucks, and of course I was right!"

"We have plenty of food here. You should come over."

"No thanks, music freaks give me hives."

I pretend I didn't hear that, too. "What are you doing later on?"

"Maybe a movie, want to go?"

"Can't. I need to practice once everybody gets out of here. Voice lesson tomorrow."

"Skip a night."

"Can't."

She sighs, long and loud. I know I'm going to get shit from her later. But with the Blackmore coming up, I can tell I'm going to have to do a better job juggling my social life and music.

"Well, call me when you're ready to join the real world," Chloe says. "I'll be waiting with all the normal people."

I hang up. Look around and . . . whatever. Chloe has no idea what she's talking about.

"Here." I hand Laura a beach ball. "I can use some extra lungs."

She blows and I blow. Awesome smells drift over from the grill. "Find Your Grail" comes on the iPod, and people launch into another sing-along. I'm enjoying the slightly dizzy sensation that blowing into this little plastic tube is giving me and then . . . I get this weird feeling. Like a tingling on the back of my neck. I look up, and there is Kathryn sitting by the side of the pool. I was so caught up in the whole *Gondoliers* thing and thinking about John Moorehouse that I didn't see her. Now I feel like I should make sure it actually is her. When you've been enemies for as long as she and I have, it's weird to see the other person in your own backyard.

The more I look, the more my good mood dissolves. I'll come right out and say it because it's pathetic to deny the obvious: Kathryn is really pretty. She's never had to put up with brothers who think it's funny to call her an Amazon or Brookehilde. She's never had to worry about being too tall or her nose being too big. All the guys look at her, and you know she knows it. But she spends all her time hanging on to Matt McWalter like he's some sort of security blanket.

"Why the sour face?"

Cold metal touches my neck. I turn around to see Brice with a long fork in one hand, a plate of grilled burgers in the other. Laura pops up in her chair and sits with her back all straight. It's obvious she wants me to introduce the two of them. Instead I say, "Trying not to lose my lunch."

They both look over at Kathryn, who's sitting with her knees smashed up against her chest. "Hey, isn't that . . . ," Brice says.

"Yeah."

"Well, somebody should go over and say hi. She looks lonely."

"Please," I say. "Don't encourage her."

"She still on your shit list?"

"She will never *not* be on my shit list."

He gives me that annoying look that says he thinks he knows me better than I know myself. I look over at Laura for a little moral support.

"Brooke isn't the only one who doesn't like her," Laura jumps in. "She's basically a leper with the whole school."

"All the more reason to stage a rescue." Brice makes a move to go over. Before he can get away, I reach up and grab the plate of burgers out of his hand. Laura squeals and jumps up, knocking over her chair.

"Leave Kathryn alone," I tell Brice. "Or I'll toss it overboard."

"You wouldn't," he says.

"Oh no?" I walk to the side of the pool and hold the burgers over the water. Suddenly the wind picks up and a beach ball rolls across the concrete from the gazebo.

I have a better idea.

"You know what?" I say. "Now that you mention it she does look kind of lonely. Why don't you get her in the water for some volleyball?"

Brice smiles. "Now *that's* what I'm talking about," he says. "I knew you were hiding Nice Brooke somewhere."

He jumps into the water and starts wading over to where Kathryn is sitting. I give Laura a little shrug before calling after him.

"Don't let her tell you she doesn't want to play! Kathryn's shy. She needs to loosen up."

KATHRYN

"HEY, KATHRYN! CATCH!" A BEACH ball hits me in the chest and then plops into my lap. I look up to see Brooke's older brother Brice bobbing in the water in front of me.

"Volleyball," he says brightly. "Come on in!"

"That's okay," I tell him. "I'm no good at it."

"I don't believe you. You tell me you suck, you get in here and prove it."

I'm torn between flustered and flattered. It's nice to be included, especially by somebody like Brice, who is something of a legend at our school. But then I wonder: Is he asking because he really wants me to play, or . . . I look over at Brooke, who is staring straight at me.

"Come on, Kathryn!" Brice says. Over his shoulder I see Brooke suddenly stride to the edge of the pool.

"I'll play!" she shouts, and dives into the deep end.

I look for Matt, but he's still on the other side of the

patio. I'm about to stand and walk away when a pair of arms grabs me about the waist. It's Tim McNamara again—I know because my nose is pressed flat up against Marvin the Martian. All I can register is mild surprise as he lifts me up and heaves me into the pool.

I hold my breath as we crash into the water. We're under only a second before Tim pulls me up and sets me on my feet. My hair is soaked, my heart racing, and my makeup is probably running down my face, but my feet are touching the bottom and the water isn't too deep, so I try to shake off the panic. I play along because now that I'm here there is no way to get out without making a scene. The splash must have caught Matt's attention because he's watching from the side now, just as trapped as me; if he tries to help, then everybody will know my secret.

They're all in the pool now, grouped on either side of a volleyball net that seems to have sprouted out of nowhere. The game gets going and I try to keep calm as people leap and dive around me, chasing the big, pink beach ball. Everything goes okay until it's Brooke's turn to serve. Her aim is impeccable—every single serve comes straight at me. The first couple of times I duck, letting somebody else lob the ball back. After a while I begin to get the hang of it, lifting my arm to smack the wet ball back over the net as people on my team cheer.

We get ready for another serve. Brooke raises the ball, and I prepare for it to come sailing in my direction. Then, at the last minute, she shifts her focus and hurls it at another girl on my team, beaning her right in the chest.

"Dodgeball!" Brooke screams, and people start hitting one another with anything they can find—balls, foam sticks, even a wet towel or two. I freeze, figuring if I stand still I can keep from getting knocked over.

I'm wrong.

Somebody snatches my legs out from under me, and I go under. I fight my way back toward the surface, and there's Brooke, wading toward me with a big, green Nerf ball. She aims it, spinning and dripping, at my head, and I turn to keep from getting hit. As I twist, I lose my footing. *Splash*—I'm under again. It's a forest of legs down here, and I think I've got my ups and downs mixed up because I can't get my feet underneath me anymore. A knee whacks me in the face and I bite down on my lip. Pink blood billows out of my mouth. I try to grab a shoulder, a hip, a hand, but everything is moving. I'm grasping, but all I get are handfuls of water. The surface shimmers just feet above my head, but I can't reach it.

"Get out of the way! Out of the way!"

I open my eyes and try to bring my hands to my face

before I realize that Matt has both of my arms around his neck as he carries me, soldier-style, out of the water. He drops me onto the pool deck as people crowd around, some looking like they're about to cry, some laughing like they haven't figured out yet what's going on. I cough and gag; I think I might throw up all over the patio. "Good thing we haven't had dinner yet," says somebody in the crowd, who gets shushed by somebody else.

Brooke's mother bursts out of the group, helps me to my feet, and rubs my back as I bend over, coughing the rest of the water out. "Are you all right, honey?" she says. "Should we take you to the emergency room?"

I shake my head, stunned. Matt takes my arm. "She's just shook up, I think. Maybe I should take her home."

"Yes, of course," says Mrs. Dempsey. "I'm so sorry the evening had to end like this. Are you sure you're all right, dear?"

Somebody gives me a washrag filled with ice for my bloody lip. "Bye, Kathryn. Bye," people say in little, sympathetic voices. Brooke is the only person still in the pool. She fixes me with an icy glare as we go by, and I have to look away, just like I always do when things between us come too close to the surface.

Mrs. Dempsey slides open the patio door and leads me into her air-conditioned kitchen. It's as if a DVD has been set on pause and somebody just hit the play button;

the cold brings my senses back and my thoughts begin to spool forward.

"I put your bag in Brooke's room," Mrs. Dempsey says, ushering me into the foyer.

"Thanks," I say, testing to see if my lip has quit bleeding. It has, and I bite again to stop it from trembling. "I can find it."

As soon as she's gone and I hear the patio door slide shut, the tears come. I swipe my arm across my eyes so I can see my way up Brooke's huge staircase.

"I'm such an idiot!" My voice hitches with rage and humiliation.

"What?" says Matt, following right behind. "What did you say?"

I speak louder, but not much, because I have no idea who else might be in the house. "I *knew* something like this was going to happen. Something like this always happens with her."

"It was just people being stupid," he says. "Come on, it's not that bad."

"Not that bad? She tried to kill me!"

"She did not try to kill you, Kath. You're taking this way too far now."

I stop at the landing and turn to look down at him. "She knows I can't swim."

He stares at me like I'm insane; I turn back around

and head down the hall toward Brooke's room, the second door on the right.

"Kath . . ."

"Matt," I say, grabbing the knob so hard that it rattles, "believe me. She knows." Then I go in and shut the door.

The tears begin to slow as I look around. It is a huge room—a suite, really, with a private bathroom and a second room off to the side where Brooke keeps a piano all her own. I take another step in. My things wait on the bed, half buried under backpacks, beach bags, and bundles of other people's clothes. I reach for my duffel but then stop.

It's strange being in someone else's personal space when they aren't there; everything has an energy to it, like a part of the person is still in the room, watching everything you do. Brooke has piles of new clothes with the tags still on them draped over her desk chair, a brand-new laptop on her desk, and an iPod on her bedside table. The room smells of an expensive perfume I tried on once at the mall.

Something yellow catches my eye—the Blackmore pamphlet, stuck to her vanity mirror with the entry form already torn out. Taped next to it are pictures of Brooke at parties, Brooke at football games, Brooke messing around with the other A-listers outside by the pool. I run my finger along the frayed edges of the pamphlet and then step away from the dresser. Matt was wrong; nothing has changed between the two of us. I survey the room once again. Nothing has changed here, either. Everything is pretty much the way I remember it. See, I've been in Brooke's room before—a long time ago, when she and I were friends.

JUNIOR YEAR

*Capriccioso: music that is free and lively yet also unpredict-
able and, at times, volatile*

BROOKE

I HEARD KATHRYN BEFORE I ever met her—through the door of a practice room freshman year, on my way to audition for Honors Choir.

For everybody else in my class, starting high school was superscary. After a summer of parties with Brice and Bill Jr., freshman year for me felt pretty much like an extension of junior high—nothing to be afraid of, but nothing to get excited about, either.

Nothing, except for music.

With my audition piece under my arm, I opened the door to the music wing and took a couple of steps inside. Ever since we'd moved to Lake Champion I'd been obsessed with the vocal department at William O. Douglas. Knowing I could go there someday was the one thing that kept me sane after my mom yanked us out of New York.

First, I stopped to check out the trophy case with the

plaques honoring all the choirs and soloists who'd won first place at State. Next to those was a line of photos showing the Honors Choir through the years. Girls in burgundy gowns stood in formation next to guys in tuxes. They looked grown-up and serious. Professional. Just like I wanted to be.

I took a sip from my water bottle and started down the hall. I walked past the practice rooms, hearing people warming up through the doors. And then I went past the door to the stage where I'd always seen the Honors Choir perform. Most of the time I'd had to go to concerts by myself because none of my friends ever wanted to go along.

As I got closer to the choir room I could hear more and more people rehearsing. I started putting my ear up to doors. And that's when I heard her—this incredible soprano voice singing "Deh Vieni Non Tardar" from *The Marriage of Figaro*. The voice was sweet but powerful. So clear and focused you could hear every word, even through the practice room door. I would have felt threatened by a voice like that, except whoever it belonged to wasn't competition since I was up for an alto spot.

"Dempsey? Brooke Dempsey?" I snapped around to see a woman poking her head out of the audition room.

"Um . . . that's me." I'd gotten so caught up listening that I'd missed my chance for a last-minute warm-up.

She held the door open while I went in. I hoped the hour I'd done at home would be enough.

Anderson sat behind a big folding table. "Brooke Dempsey," he said. "Why does that name sound familiar?" He looked through my paperwork while the rest of the judges stared at me. For a second I panicked, thinking maybe they'd heard about how I'd gotten wasted at the Fourth of July party and almost got arrested trying to climb the water tower by the lake, or how I threw up all over the lobby of the Steak 'n' Shake when Chloe and I got the beer munchies two weeks after that.

"Ah yes," Anderson said. He'd found my Training and Experience sheet. "You study with Hildy Shultz, over at the university—she mentioned you to me."

"She really respects the program here," I told him. I hoped I didn't sound like an ass kisser.

Anderson just nodded and said, "Are you familiar with how we structure our choruses?"

I nodded, almost laughing. I knew everything there was to know about how the department worked. I knew that most people started out in freshman glee club or Concert Choir, and then worked their way up through Chorale and into Honors Choir at the top. Usually only juniors and seniors got into Honors. Sometimes a sophomore made it, but freshmen almost never got in.

I'd made up my mind that I would be different.

"What are you going to sing for us?" Anderson said.

"'Che faro senza Euridice,' by Gluck."

"Impressive. Begin when you're ready."

I took a second. Shut my eyes and got focused. Then I nodded for the pianist to start the introduction. To this day I still remember it as one of those performances where everything goes right. The notes just came without me having to think about them. I even took a chance on a cadenza at the end and nailed it.

Anderson told me, "Excellent. Check the results tomorrow, then enroll in the appropriate class when you come to school on Monday."

As I left the room a tiny girl was standing by the door, waiting to go in next. I watched her through the window as she gave her music to the accompanist. Then she started to sing. The door blocked most of the sound, but I could hear enough. It was her—the soprano from before.

And so it turned out I wasn't the only freshman who made it into Honors. Kathryn showed up, too, sitting a few seats away from me in the back row. I recognized her by the long, dark hair. But even though we were considered freaks and intruders by the upperclassmen, and even though I knew how good a singer she was, we never talked. Our school is huge, and I always had stuff going on with Bill and Brice's friends. It wasn't until the twins graduated, leaving me and Chloe without an automatic social life, that I really got to know Kathryn.

Chloe noticed her when she came to meet me after choir on the first day of junior year.

"Who's that?" said Chloe.

I looked where she was pointing, and there was Kathryn, walking away from us down the hall.

"Her name's Kathryn," I said. "Pease, maybe?"

"She's pretty," said Chloe.

A light went on in her eyes, and I could see the ideas start to bubble up. Chloe's the social director in our group—sort of like a teenage Martha Stewart, Miss Manners, and Perez Hilton, all rolled up in one. Back in sixth grade, she was the first person who put into words why people were so interested in a gawky new girl from New York. *You're popular, Brooke,* she'd told me. *You're lucky.* When we got to William O. Douglas, she'd made herself the official keeper of the A-list for our class—no one was admitted without Chloe's blessing.

"We should invite that girl out," Chloe said. "In fact, I can think of a lot of people we should invite out. Now that your brothers are gone we should be recruiting new friends. No. Wait. We should be *discovering* them!" She got out her notebook and started scribbling. "We'll have a slumber party. It'll be like sorority rush!"

"I don't know," I said. "Won't it be weird walking up to people and saying, 'Here, come to my house so we can ogle you all night'?"

"It won't be weird, it'll be great." Chloe handed me what she'd written. *Meet new friends Friday night at our JUNIOR GIRLS SLUMBER PARTY!!!* "I'll make invites tonight," she said. "Quit frowning, Brooke, this is going to be fun."

The invitations, which Chloe printed on Pepto-pink paper, made it obvious what the slumber party was really for. Especially when you looked at who got one and who didn't. Chloe started with our basic group of friends. Then she filled out the guest list with girls she'd seen in the hallways and in class. The main criterion for getting invited was "looks cool."

"What does that mean?" I said as I went over the guest list with her in the commons after school.

"You know." She waved at a couple of girls walking past like they were animals at the zoo. "Pretty. Nice clothes. Like that girl from your choir—what's her name? Kassie?"

"Kathryn."

"Right. Like her."

"Kathryn doesn't have nice clothes." Kathryn actually had great clothes. But they weren't brand names.

A lot of her stuff looked handmade—skirts sewn out of vintage fabric, hand-knit sweaters. You couldn't find stuff like that at the mall.

"She's got inner style," Chloe told me. "It's a wonder the music freaks haven't killed it yet."

Chloe sat down on a bench and started rummaging through her purse.

"I'm a music freak," I told her.

"No, you're not." She pulled a big purple pen out of her bag and started adding names to the list. "You're superinvolved."

"What's that supposed to mean?" I bent over and took her notebook away so she'd have to look me in the eye. Chloe knew how much music meant to me.

She sighed and tossed her razored red hair. "You're one of those people that does it all. You have to be a little bit into everything. If you weren't you'd only be a little bit popular."

"But I'm not a little bit into music," I said. "That's what I do."

"Well, thank God you do other things, too." She grabbed the notebook and went back to her list.

The original plan was for us to have the party at Chloe's house. Her stepdad, who was in the middle of running for state representative, had just put in a new hot tub, and she was dying to show it off. But then he invited some big campaign donors over for dinner. Chloe's mom waited until that morning to tell her our party would be too disruptive, and, by the way, could she please make herself scarce for the rest of the evening?

I thought it sounded like a great excuse to cancel. But Chloe wanted to have the party more than ever, so we went to plan B. We had it at my place. She had Dina Mendoza text out the new plans, conveniently neglecting to mention that my mom would be working late. Not that it really mattered. Even when Mom was around, she always pretty much let the twins do whatever they wanted, and that extended to me, too.

"Easy on the onions!" Chloe shouted. She swooped down on Angela Van Zant, who was making chili at the stove in my kitchen. "Seriously, An! We don't want our breath to reek while we're talking to people."

"Sorry," said Angela, and she started scooping onions out of the pot.

I hoisted myself onto the counter and stole a carrot from the veggie tray. "Why don't you make it yourself, Rachael Ray? Then you can put in whatever you want."

"Because it's inefficient," said Chloe. She took the spoon from Angela and removed all but the last few pieces of onion. "Everybody has a job to do, and if everybody would do it *right*, then we wouldn't be running late like we are right now."

I looked around and, sure enough, Chloe had taken a bunch of our friends and put them to work. We'd already dragged the flat screen up to my room, plus the Wii. Now we were making refreshments. Jenna Rogers and Kiersten Coons were in charge of cutting up veggies while Madison Verbeck spooned cookie dough onto baking sheets. Violet Alexander was mixing up guacamole, and . . .

"Where's Dina?" I asked just as Bill and Brice banged into the kitchen. College hadn't started for them yet, so they'd stayed in Lake Champion an extra week to party. Their arms were loaded with bags from the liquor store that never checks IDs.

As soon as they saw the twins, everybody dropped what they were doing and tried to look cool.

"So, Bill!" chirped Chloe. "Are you two going to be around tonight? We could totally use your input on the new girls."

"That's a negative." Bill leaned over and snagged a celery stick. "We're headed to The Rocks."

"But we didn't forget you," added Brice. He set one of his bags down on the table. "There's beer, Boone's, and peach schnapps in there. Should be enough to at least get you started."

Everybody totally forgot their cool as they swarmed

around the table. If it's possible to fit fourteen arms into one paper bag, we managed to do it. I opened a bottle of beer and took a long drink.

"Hey, Brooke." Brice stopped on his way out the door. "How's your ass?"

"Yeah!" chimed in Bill before they both disappeared down the hall. "Watch your butt tonight, okay, Baby B?"

Everybody cracked up. I poured the rest of my beer down the sink. At the end-of-summer party, I'd thought it was hilarious to let Dan Hummel chase me around and try to whip my bare ass with some old Mardi Gras beads we'd found in my kitchen junk drawer. The next morning, though, when my butt cheeks were covered in welts and people were posting photos on Facebook, it didn't seem funny at all. Plus, I had a hazy memory of running into the street and almost getting hit by a car. All because I was sloppy, stupid drunk.

I tossed my bottle into the recycle bin, but if anybody noticed me wasting perfectly good beer they didn't say anything. That's because Dina had just walked into the room.

"Dina!" shouted Chloe. "Where are the DVDs? Didn't you get them?"

"No." Dina's voice was small and sad. She slumped into a kitchen chair.

"Hey!" I went over and knelt down next to her. "What happened?"

"I went to Videoworld."

"And?" Videoworld was a dump, but not bad enough for a visit there to make someone look borderline suicidal. Dina glanced around to see if the others were listening. They totally were, even though they pretended to be busy with their snack making.

"*He* works at Videoworld," she half-whispered to me. "I didn't know he worked there."

"What? Oh no!" Chloe flew across the kitchen and flung her arms around Dina's neck. "Are you saying you saw Noah?"

Dina deflated even more. Her nose went red.

"I didn't know he worked there, either!" Chloe said. "If I'd known I would have told you to go to Blockbuster instead. It's just that Videoworld has such a better selection. . . ."

I shot Chloe a look. Noah Brink was a senior. Dina'd practically gone all the way with him over the summer and he'd not only dumped her the next week, but he'd told everybody the gory details, too. Dina had been avoiding Noah like the plague ever since.

"That must have been awful," Chloe murmured. "Especially after you sent him that email with your class schedule so the two of you would never even have to be in the same hallway."

"You did?" said Madison from over by the oven.

"I have to go to the bathroom," said Dina. She jumped up and hurried out of the room. I rolled my eyes. *This* was why you never told Chloe anything you didn't want broadcast to the rest of the world in bold-face caps.

"Are you sure you didn't know he worked there?" I asked. Chloe'd been mad at Dina for going to lunch with the cheerleaders and not inviting her along. And since Chloe always knew everything, it wasn't hard to imagine she also knew where the guy who'd broken Dina's heart worked.

"I swear. I had no idea." Chloe looked seriously sorry. "I'll go talk to her."

"No, I'll do it," I said. With Chloe's big mouth, she'd probably do more harm than good.

"Hey," I called through the bathroom door. "Dina, it's okay. We'll do pay-per-view tonight. Or we don't even need videos. We're supposed to be meeting people, not watching movies, right?" I heard sniffling, then the faucet. Dina opened the door. Her eyes were still red, but she didn't look so miserable. "Don't think about it for the rest of the night," I told her. "At least you're here partying and he's stuck at work."

She smiled, nodded, and let me lead her back into

the kitchen. Jenna offered Dina her knife. "Wanna help cut the cauliflower?"

Dina took the knife and started cutting neat little flowerettes while Violet smashed avocados, Madison kept an eye on her cookies, and Angela watched Chloe stir the chili.

A few minutes later, the doorbell rang.

"Okay. This is it!" said Chloe. She whipped off her apron. "Whoever you talk to, remember as much as you can so you can report back afterward!"

Everybody showed up at once, it seemed like. All of a sudden my foyer was filled with girls we barely knew, all of them looking overdressed and nervous. Chloe raised her eyebrow at me as she took purses and overnight bags. She was enjoying it all way too much. I'd just started to get claustrophobic when I saw a brown ponytail through the crowd. It was Kathryn, getting cornered by Angela with Twenty Questions.

I went over to rescue her.

"Sorry about this," I said as I helped stick a name tag onto her baby blue sweater. The sweater had a little pearl flower on the chest and looked like it came from a vintage shop. "Some people suck at remembering names."

"That's okay." Her eyes had little gold specks that flickered when she looked at me. "I could use some help, too."

"Listen up, please!" Chloe reappeared on the stairs, clinking a water glass with a knife. "Thanks so much for coming tonight, everyone. We've got dinner and refreshments in the kitchen, if you'd like to follow me in there."

We wound up standing around the table trying to ignore the rumbling in our stomachs. The chili on the stove smelled great, but nobody ate anything. I could see the rest of our friends sending ESP messages back and forth across the table: *What do you think about this one? Is she good enough? Is she too good?* Meanwhile, the new girls were talking over one another, trying too hard. Kathryn caught me watching and smiled.

Finally, Chloe made everybody go up to my room. We sat in a circle on the floor and passed the schnapps around, the new girls trying not to make faces as they took huge gulps. The alcohol did what it was supposed to do. Before long, people were talking, laughing, and dancing around the room to old Madonna songs.

I went downstairs to bring up the chili. When I got back, Kathryn was standing off by herself, flipping through my CDs.

"Having fun?" I said. I hoped she'd say no so I could launch a rant about how fake the whole evening was. Something about Kathryn made me think she'd understand.

"I'm having a great time," she said. "Your friends are nice."

I put the chili down on my desk. Who was I kidding? Nobody was going to eat it.

"Tell me you're just saying that."

"Okay, I'm just saying that." Kathryn laughed a quiet little laugh and held up a collection of French art songs. "Dawn Upshaw. I love her."

"Me too. My dad took me to see her in *The Great Gatsby* at the Met. It was amazing."

Kathryn's eyes got wide. "You've been to the Met?"

"Sure. Haven't you?"

"I've never been to New York. My mom and I were saving up to go over spring break but it's so expensive. I listen to the operas every Saturday on the radio, though."

I couldn't believe it. I'd thought I was the only person who did that.

"So what did you think about the new *Turandot*?" I'd been dying to talk about it ever since the broadcast.

"The new aria was great, but I couldn't handle that it didn't end with 'Nessun Dorma.' I guess I'm traditional that way."

"Totally." I couldn't stop staring at her. Nobody I knew knew anything about music, let alone a famous melody from a Puccini opera.

Chloe had opened my closet and the other girls

were trying on my clothes. Kathryn laughed as Violet flounced around in my old Halloween flapper boa. "Mr. Lieb, my voice teacher at Baldwin, says not listening to the Met is like wasting a free ticket."

"That's what Hildy says, too. Lieb has his studio off the courtyard, right? Hildy Schultz is right down the hall."

Kathryn nodded and flipped some more. "You have a really good collection."

"Dawn Upshaw is my only soprano. I'm all about the mezzos and contraltos. Listen to this."

I took Madonna out of the CD player and popped in Bizet's *Carmen*. Denyce Graves singing "Down Near the Walls of Sevilla" came blaring out of the speakers. Kathryn tipped her head and nodded along with the music. "Denyce Graves is awesome," she said. "Did you see her in *Aida* in St. Paul?"

"Hey!" Chloe's voice came at us from across the room. "Turn that crap off!" She grabbed a couple of the new girls, whirled them around to face me, and announced, "Brooke here wants to be an opera singer when she grows up. Which is fine and all, as long as the rest of us don't have to hear it."

Kathryn ejected the CD and handed it to me. "Maybe we can listen some other time," she said.

I took the CD and smiled a smile that said, *See, Chloe?*

Somebody else cares about this stuff, too.

"Fine," I said. "But one of these days you'll wish you were nicer to us music freaks."

Chloe waved a *whatever* hand as she turned away.

"I highly doubt that," she said.

KATHRYN

TWO HOURS. THAT'S HOW MUCH sleep I
got the night of the slumber party, just two hours somewhere between four in the morning and ten a.m., when
I stumbled back through my own front door, headachy,
stale-mouthed, and utterly exhilarated. All of the years
that I'd kept to myself with Matt, I'd convinced myself
I wasn't missing anything; Matt was comfortable and
familiar, just like the best guy friends in the old movies
we liked to watch, and that was good enough for me. I
didn't need girlfriends.

After Brooke's, however, I knew it wasn't true. There
was something special about being around other girls,
a sense of belonging I'd never experienced before. And
I *did* belong—at least that's how it felt, because everybody seemed to be going out of their way to make it easy.
Dina, Chloe, Angela . . . I could recall faces and voices,
but I couldn't remember all of their names. The only

person who stood out as a clear, fully formed person was Brooke, mostly because I'd already noticed her in choir—it was impossible not to, with her deep voice and her easy confidence. Even when we were freshmen and technically supposed to be keeping our heads down and paying our dues, she talked and joked around with the upperclassmen like she'd known them forever.

I soon found out that she probably had.

"Do you know who her brothers are?" Matt asked me when I showed him the pink slumber party invitation. "Bill and Brice Dempsey."

"Really?" I hadn't been completely under a rock for the past two years; I knew about the golden twins who'd practically ruled the school before graduating the previous spring.

"People are still talking about them," Matt told me. "And it looks like Brooke is going to inherit all of it."

I reread the invitation as if the words were a new language to learn. "So why does she want me, I wonder?"

"Because you're amazing." He pulled a face of mock terror. "Oh noes! What if you become insanely popular? I'll be so lonely!"

"Don't worry," I said, folding the pink paper and tucking it inside my aria book. "I somehow doubt I'll be deemed worthy."

But the amazing thing about that night was the feeling that I *was* worthy. Riding home from Brooke's party in my father's car, I switched the radio from the morning news to a pop station, and as we rounded the corner onto our street a song came on that I had danced to just hours earlier. Dad let me listen in the driveway until it was over, even though he needed to leave for a job fair.

"Wish me luck, Sweetpea?" he'd said as I gathered up my things. He wore his business suit, which made me sad every time I saw it. At his last job he only ever wore short sleeves and khakis; nerdy, but I preferred nerdy to formal. Formal meant résumés and waiting for interview callbacks and Mom working longer hours, clipping coupons, and staying up all night worrying.

"Good luck," I said, and kissed him on the cheek.

Inside the house, Mom sat on the living room couch with her coffee and her morning crossword puzzle spread out across her lap.

"There you are!" she said. "I didn't know when to expect you."

"It's not that late." I ran my tongue over my teeth, hoping my breath didn't smell like peach schnapps.

"Not late at all. It's just you have your first English paper due this week. I thought you'd want to get started on it."

"I'm going to work on it now," I told her. My eyes were sandy and my brain felt sluggish from lack of sleep.

"Great!" she said. "Do you want some coffee to help you stay awake?"

She loaded me down with an old French press, a mug, and a plate of buttered toast, then she sent me upstairs, but instead of going to the guest room where we keep the computer, I went to my own room across the hall and lay down on the bed. I closed my eyes and let my mind fill with images—Brooke's elegant house, her brothers coming home at three a.m. and entertaining us with stories about the party they'd just attended, the other girls in their pajamas, dancing around Brooke's room like actors in a TV commercial. We'd polished one another's nails. We'd chatted online with some sophomore guys, giggling when they mooned the webcam. We'd seen one another in our underwear, retainers, and zit cream; I fell asleep with these things in my mind.

Three hours later, I woke up to the phone ringing.

"Kathryn!" my mom shouted from downstairs. "It's for you!"

I stumbled into the computer room, grateful she hadn't seen me sleeping, and groped around for the cordless. I thought it would be Matt but it wasn't; my face flushed as I listened to Brooke's voice on the other end of the line.

"I've got tickets to the operettas at Baldwin tonight," she said. "It's Vaughan Williams and Gilbert and Sullivan. *Riders to the Sea* and *Trial by Jury*. Want to go?"

"Really?" I checked the caller ID window to make sure it wasn't a prank.

"Yeah, really. The lead in *Trial* is one of Lieb's prize sopranos. Don't you want to hear what your teacher's other students sound like?"

"Uh-huh . . ." I smacked myself on the forehead, hoping it would knock out something more intelligent.

"Cool," said Brooke. "We'll pick you up at six thirty. Give me your address. I'll get directions online."

"Who was that?" Mom asked as I hung up. She'd come to take my dishes back downstairs and looked puzzled to find them on my bedroom dresser, untouched.

"Brooke Dempsey," I told her. "The girl whose house I went to last night. She invited me to see some operas."

Mom looked worried. "You're going out again? Tonight? What about your paper?"

"I'll get up early tomorrow and write it. I'll have a draft done before church. Promise."

She looked at the cold coffee and toast, then at the computer, which, I realized with a silent groan, hadn't even been turned on. "I want you home by eleven," she said. "And no going out tomorrow, even if it's with Matt."

"I don't have plans for tomorrow, and I don't have any plans to make plans." I was starting to get antsy; I had a lot to do before Brooke came to pick me up. "You don't have to worry, Mom. I'll get the paper done."

One last look of concern, and she headed back downstairs. I listened for her footfalls on the first-floor landing, then I ran back into my room and threw open the closet door. With all that had happened in the past twelve hours I guess I expected my wardrobe to be transformed, too, but what I found in there depressed me completely. I don't have a lot of money for clothes; most of what I have I either buy from thrift shops or my mom makes. She gets fabric from vintage stores when it's not too expensive, and from the craft shop where she works. She's good enough to copy what we see on TV and in magazines without needing a pattern, still it's never quite the same as what the other kids are wearing.

After trying on everything even remotely appropriate, I settled on a black skirt with a sweater that she'd knitted for my birthday the year before. I took a shower and did my hair and makeup. Then, partly to keep Mom happy and mostly to keep my mind off the waiting, I hammered out an outline for my English paper, eating dinner in front of the computer. I kept checking the little clock in the corner of the screen, watching the minutes tick down to six thirty and past. *She meant to ask somebody else,* I told myself, trying not to be disappointed as I watched the clock creep toward six forty-five. *It's nothing personal.*

Then I heard a car in the driveway. I looked out the guest room window to see Brooke's mom behind the wheel of a new SUV with Brooke in the passenger seat.

"Going now! Back by eleven!" I shouted as I ran down the stairs and out the front door.

"Nice sweater," said Brooke as I slid into the back-seat. Immediately, I wished I'd picked something else. The yarn was lumpy, the sweater smelled musty—it was all wrong and Brooke had noticed. But then she turned around and said, "That's really cool. It's like ten times more sophisticated than the crap at the mall."

With Brooke in front of me, I had a good view of her outfit as well: a suede skirt, wrap sweater, and powerful-looking knee-high boots; when we got to Baldwin, she blended right in with the college kids. Around her neck she wore a silver star pendant that sparkled against her tanned skin. She even smelled nice—like green tea and cucumber. Sitting next to her in the small theater at the university arts center, I felt almost as if I were on a date.

The operettas ended and we left campus for a coffee shop down the street. "Just for some herbal tea," Brooke told me. "Caffeine's terrible for your voice."

We sat with our mugs at a table near the window and watched the college kids wander in and out. After a while the silence made me nervous, and I started searching for conversation topics.

"So . . . what did you think of the operas?" I asked.

She bobbed the tea bag in her cup, thinking. "I liked the baritone and I'm not usually a fan. But overall I think the conservatory is getting overrated."

"My teacher says the singers were a lot better when he first started working here."

"That's what Hildy says, too. She doesn't even get mad anymore when I go back to New York for lessons."

I couldn't believe how confident she was—the way she talked about New York, like it was someplace people jetted off to on any ordinary day.

"So does that mean you're not going to college at Baldwin?" I asked.

"Are you kidding? The second I'm done at Douglas I'm out of here. The only reason I'm not in a rubber room right now is because we've got the Blackmore next year."

"Mr. Lieb . . ." I cleared my throat. Brooke called her voice teacher by her first name, and I didn't want to sound like a baby. "I mean, David—he's already talking about repertoire and competition strategies."

"You have to start thinking about it early," she said. "You went last year, right?"

I nodded, remembering. "Cameron Bell." The name came out like a sigh.

Brooke sighed, too. "He showed up from some tiny

town nobody ever heard of and just blew everybody away."

"And now he's singing at Chicago Lyric."

"Exactly." Brooke played with the star around her neck, twirling it between her fingers. "My dad has an apartment on the Upper West Side. If I don't get in at Juilliard, I'll live with him. Take a year to train and then start the audition circuit."

"You're serious about singing for a career."

"Totally. Aren't you?"

I gazed into my teacup and thought about my parents. Out of all my activities, music probably offered the best shot at a scholarship, but none of us had given much thought to what might come after that.

"I don't know," I said. "I think I'll be happy just to get away, you know? There's too much pressure here to be something I'm not even sure I want to be."

Brooke nodded. "I know exactly what you mean."

We were quiet again, me sipping my tea while Brooke hummed part of the Gilbert and Sullivan to herself. When some of the operetta singers came in and started to gossip, she and I had the same idea at the same time; we grabbed magazines and pretended to read them while we eavesdropped, grinning at each other over the glossy pages.

"This is really cool," Brooke whispered. "None of my

other friends will do this kind of stuff with me."

I didn't know what to say; I ducked my head behind my magazine to hide my reddening cheeks. Those words had put a twinge in my chest—a new feeling, like happiness mingled with fear:

Brooke Dempsey, the most popular girl in my class, had called me her friend.

BROOKE

"EARTH TO BROOKE. COME IN, Brooke...."

Chloe's voice snapped me back to the commons. Back to the bench by the window where all our friends used to hang out. "Sorry," I said. "What were we talking about?"

"I'm on a mission," said Chloe.

"A new one?"

"Yep." She leaned in so the rest of us would have to lean in, too. "Two words: Senior Keg."

"But only seniors go to Senior Keg," said Dina.

"I've been doing my research. Last year Claire Dennison went because she was going out with Skip Miller. And the year before that, the JV cheer squad got to go because they'd worked up some stupid routine to do around the bonfire." Chloe paused for dramatic effect. "None of those people have what we have."

"What is that?" said Madison.

"Brooke's brothers. I bet they'd totally come back

for Senior Keg—especially if Brooke asks really, really nicely." Chloe sat back, looking very satisfied with herself.

Everybody looked at me like it was a total no-brainer, and why hadn't I thought of it myself?

"I don't think so," I said. "I'm probably going to have other plans."

Chloe shook her head. "You're not telling me this, Brooke. Do not mess with my mission."

"Then ask them yourself. You don't always have to have me with you."

Chloe opened a container of yogurt and stabbed her spoon into it. "You always have other plans these days. What's she like?"

"Who?"

"That girl from the party. Kristen."

"Kathryn."

"Right. You're constantly hanging out with her."

"Not really," I said. But it was stupid to try and lie. Kathryn and I had been hanging out almost every day. She'd come to my house after school and we'd listen to CDs or sing duets from my mom's old sheet music collection. Or we'd head over to Baldwin. Sneak into recitals, then go spend the evening at the coffee shop. Kathryn wasn't like other people at school who glommed onto me from the minute I walked in the building until the minute I went to bed at night. She never came over without being invited. She didn't kiss my brothers' butts. Plus, she knew how to keep secrets instead of putting everything out there like everybody else. It made it cooler when she did share. Like one day, when she showed me some stories she'd written in her journal. One was about an opera singer who loses her voice to throat cancer but still manages to get famous by swimming Lake Superior. She said the story was inspired by me, because "you never let anything hold you back." But all I could think of was that I'd been holding back for years, downplaying my music—downplaying who I really was—so the rest of my friends wouldn't give me grief about it.

"Speaking of Kathryn," said Chloe, "there she is!" Chloe jumped up so fast she almost tipped the rest of us off the bench. Kathryn was standing across the commons, in line at the Coke machines. "Let's get her over here."

"No!" I jumped up, too. Chloe and I wound up chest-to-chest. She raised an eyebrow. "It's just that we have choir," I explained. "We're supposed to get there early for warm-ups."

I picked up my bag and broke away. Never mind that we actually had choir fifth period—Chloe wouldn't remember something like that.

At least I hoped she wouldn't.

"Hey!" Kathryn said when I grabbed her arm. She'd barely finished paying for her bottled water.

"Bring that to the music wing," I told her. "I want you to hear the new *Traviata* I just downloaded."

"Okay . . ." She trotted along as we sped around the corner and pushed through the music wing doors. "I actually wanted to ask you something," she said. "Can you come over on Saturday for dinner? My mom's making a roast."

I slowed down and let go of her arm.

"Your mom cooks?"

"Yes," said Kathryn. "Doesn't yours?"

"I guess, if you call heating up a burrito cooking. She thinks anything where you have to boil water is a big deal."

"Well, Saturday is a special occasion. Usually we're not so fancy, but this is for my birthday."

My shoulders went all tight, the way they always do when I've forgotten something. "You never told me it was your birthday."

"I don't make a big deal about it," she said. "I guess I get scared nobody will care and then I'll be disappointed—or maybe they will care and then I won't know how to handle the attention. Is that weird?"

I wanted to tell her that yes, it was weird, but the

truth is that I liked being the only person she'd told. Kathryn was the kind of person who was alone a lot. Nobody ever left me alone.

Hanging out with her, we could be alone together.

Kathryn lives across town in a neighborhood that was built back in the seventies. The houses are mostly split-levels with tiny yards and trees that are all the same height. Kathryn's house is on one of the nicer streets, and it looks like it was built to look old. It has two stories, shutters on the windows, and a little porch on the front.

When Mom dropped me off a man was in the front yard, running a Weed Eater around a little flower bed.

"Hey, there!" he said as he turned off the machine. "You must be Kathryn's friend. Is it Brooke?"

He had dark hair like hers and the same sort of surprised-looking eyes. I said, "Yeah," and went to shake hands, because my mom would have given me crap later on for being rude, but also because he just looked like the kind of guy you'd want to shake hands with. He was all sweaty and dusty with grass stains on his white socks. Earlier that day, my own dad had sent me an email. He told me he and Jake were going on vacation before Jake's next movie. Someplace tropical. I'd been thinking maybe he'd come to Lake Champion to see me.

"I hear you're a singer, too," said Kathryn's dad. "And a swimmer. What do you swim?"

"Two hundred-yard freestyle." He let go of my hand, and I made myself quit obsessing about Dad and Jake—if I couldn't control it, then I needed to let it go. "Relay, too."

"I did relay back in college." He put his fingers on his tricep and squeezed the puny muscles. "Not that you'd know it now."

"Hey, Dad." Kathryn came out on the porch. "Mom says we're eating in a half hour. She wants you cleaned up."

"Thanks, Sweetpea." He winked at me and restarted the Weed Eater.

"Sorry if he tried to talk your head off," Kathryn said as we stepped into her living room. It led right into the dining room, which led straight back to the kitchen. The house felt lived in. Used and homey. I liked it.

"Come upstairs," she said. "It's nicer in my room."

She led me up the staircase to a room that barely held the bed and a dresser. I waited for her to close the door. Then I handed her the package I'd brought. She unwrapped one end and gasped as she pulled out a long shoe box. Inside was a pair of knee-high black boots.

"Oh my God," she said.

"Do you like them? I tried to get something that would

go with everything."

"I can't accept these."

"Sure you can. We can exchange them if they don't fit."

"But they're so nice," she said, running her fingertips along the leather. "I needed something like this. Was it obvious?"

"Well . . ." I hesitated. Chloe thought Kathryn had inner style, but I knew it was probably because she couldn't afford much else. "Don't think I'm trying to make you feel bad. Because your clothes are really awesome. But shoes are like the one thing you can't fake."

"I know." She buried her face in her hands. "I must look like an idiot."

I sighed. "Where in 'your clothes are really awesome' did you hear 'looks like an idiot'?"

"Okay," she said, and blushed. "I'm sorry."

"I'd kill for some of the stuff you've got."

"Really?"

"Totally. The shoes are just the finishing touch—my way of putting the icing on the birthday cake."

She put the boots on and admired herself in the closet mirror. Downstairs, I could hear pots and pans banging. The house was starting to smell great, like slow-cooked meat and fresh bread. Through the window over Kathryn's bed, I could see her father cutting the grass. Just like any normal dad on a Saturday afternoon. My dad had never mowed a lawn in his life.

"What does he do?" I asked.

"He's an engineer. A surveyor, but he got laid off a few weeks ago."

"Oh," I said. "I'm sorry."

"It's okay. He's thinking maybe he'll get another job soon."

"He seems nice."

She pulled a skirt from her closet and held it up to herself, seeing how it looked with the boots. "He's okay, I guess."

"You don't get along?"

"We get along fine, he's just . . ." She sat on the bed and started to unzip the boots. "All of the firms in town get slow and then they have layoffs, and it always seems to be him they're letting go. I feel bad when it happens, but then he's around a lot more than other dads would be, and he and my mom focus so much on my school stuff already that it's just hard. It's like I dread when he's out of work, because then it puts even more pressure on me, you know?"

I wanted to sympathize, but all I could think of was that she was crazy. Having my dad around all of the time was one of my biggest dreams.

"Plus, he's a little corny," she added. "I mean, he still

calls me Sweetpea, like he thinks I'm four years old or something."

"But that's cute," I said. "Hold on." My BlackBerry had started to vibrate. I slid it out of my pocket and checked the screen.

C.Romelli: Where r u, B?

I hit delete. Two seconds later it buzzed again. This time I ignored it.

"Don't you want to get that?" Kathryn asked.

"Nah," I said. "It's nobody." Chloe had been chasing me around ever since Monday morning, when she'd hatched her Senior Keg plan. So far I'd managed to stay a few steps ahead, but every day there were more messages.

On the phone: "Brooke, it's Chloe. Where've you been? Call me."

In my email: OK, avoid me if you want. But you just don't want to admit our party was a success. We won't bite your new friend, you know. See you tomorrow? I better!!! -C-

On IM:

CHLOECAT: Brooke?

CHLOECAT: B?

CHLOECAT: U there?

CHLOECAT: This hiding out crap? Getting old.
CHLOECAT: GROW UP!!!
CHLOECAT: Call me.

And in texts, which by that point were getting pretty pissy. Another one came through while I was helping Kathryn put the tissue paper back inside the boots.

C.Romelli: Traitor!!! ☹

I shut off the phone and stuffed it in the bottom of my purse, then I went back to spying on Kathryn's dad. I knew why Chloe wanted to reach me. She couldn't stand that I had a new best friend. But I didn't want to share Kathryn. Chloe would never appreciate her the way I did.

Peeking around the curtains, I watched Mr. Pease finish the curbs. He turned off the mower and rolled it away toward the garage. A few minutes later, the front door slammed. Footsteps came up the stairs and went into the bathroom at the end of the hall. The shower started.

"Don't you ever help him out?" I asked. "You could run the leaf blower or something."

Kathryn looked like the idea had never occurred to her. Before she could answer, her mom yelled up from the bottom of the stairs. "Kathryn, Brooke, come help me set the table!"

Kathryn's mom made an amazing dinner. And no matter what Kathryn said, her dad wasn't corny. It was just obvious he really loved his family, the way he gave her nicknames and wanted to hear about our school stuff. Kathryn blushed all through the meal, and once she told him, "Please, Dad! Let Brooke eat!" But mostly, the three of them looked really comfortable in their cozy dining room.

When she walked me to the door later on, I asked what she was doing for the rest of the evening.

"I don't know," she said. "Maybe Matt will come over and watch TV if this online thing he's hosting ever ends."

"Of course he will."

Her face went bright red. "He's just a friend."

"Whatever. He's totally in love with you." As if she hadn't noticed. It was obvious to anybody with eyes. But Kathryn just shook her head.

"And *I'm* totally changing the subject," she said. "What are *you* doing tonight?"

"Practicing."

She sighed. "That's what I should be doing."

"So do it."

"But there's TV! And Matt coming over! Why don't

you stay here and hang out with us?"

"I've gotta get my hour in. Two if I'm on a roll."

"Fine, Miss Dedicated." She handed me my purse and opened the door just as my mom was pulling up. "Go home and practice."

And I did go. And I did plan on practicing. But then Bud Dawes called, inviting me and the twins, who were home yet again, to a party at his house. I told him no. I couldn't. I had work I needed to do. And he told me Miles Monaghan would be there.

Twenty minutes later I was in my bathroom, trying to follow the directions from *InStyle* magazine on how to apply blush so as to "minimize unflattering features"—namely, my nose.

"Dempsey cab service!" Bill hollered from down the hall. "Leaving in five minutes!"

I gave up on the blush and fluffed out my hair the best I could. Then I put on the outfit I'd picked out: a gold draped sweater, jeans, and heels.

"Hey." Brice poked his head in. He looked me up and down. "You ready, Brookehilde?"

I took off the heels and put on flats instead.

"Ready."

When we got to Boodawg's house it wasn't packed, which surprised me because usually his parties are huge. This was a small group. Mostly basketball players and a few other A-listers. Looking around, I felt better—like I hadn't skipped out on practicing to go to a big bash or anything, so that made it okay.

What made it even better was Miles, in the kitchen, pumping drinks from a keg under the gourmet island.

"Brooke! Excellent!" He smiled his adorable crooked smile at me. "I told the Big Bs not to bother coming unless they brought you along."

His bangs kept falling into his eyes, which were this amazing shade of blue. He had on a navy sweater that made them look even bluer. Miles was a senior. A good friend of Bill's and Brice's. But he was different from the other guys who hung out at our house. Whenever the twins started calling me Amazon or Brookehilde, he would tell them to shut up. And he never called me Baby B. I could tell Miles didn't go for girls who were just pretty. Miles wanted something different. Someone special.

Miles Monaghan, I had decided, would be my first real boyfriend.

I hadn't told anybody about it. Not even Kathryn, which was kind of dumb, because if I was going to tell anybody, it would have been her. Maybe I felt weird because I'd never had a boyfriend before. Mostly, though, I think it was just because I wanted to wait until I actually had something to talk about.

"Want a beer?" Miles asked me.

"No thanks," I said. "I don't drink."

"As of when?"

"As of now." I prayed he wouldn't bring up the scene with Dan Hummel and the Mardi Gras beads. Or all the other times he'd seen me doing stupid stuff while trashed on crappy keg beer.

"Then soda it is," he said. "Care to join me in the living room?"

Boodawg had a fire in his parents' fireplace, and I sat in a big leather chair while Miles took the ottoman. We talked about swimming. About whether I should run for student council. About people who were at the party and people who weren't. He drank his beer, getting looser as he reached the bottom. His eyelids were starting to droop. He leaned in closer. His bangs were in his eyes, and I kept wanting to reach up and brush them away.

All of a sudden, cold air went across the back of my neck. Somebody had walked in the front door. Miles looked over my shoulder.

"Chloe's here," he said. "Who's that with her?"

I turned around, and there was Kathryn.

She had on a sixties-looking wrap dress that probably really was from the sixties. Her hair was down around her shoulders, which I had never seen before. She always wore it in a ponytail when we hung out. On her feet were the boots I had given her for her birthday. Chloe and Dina each had an arm, and they were showing her off, introducing her to everybody they ran into. Kathryn looked a little overwhelmed, but she smiled and went along with it. If you didn't know her, you'd never know just how shy she could be.

I got up. "Wait here," I told Miles. Then I went over to where the three of them were giving Boodawg their coats.

"Hey!" Kathryn looked surprised to see me. "I thought you were going home to practice."

"I thought *you* were ordering pizza with Matt."

She took off her scarf and handed it to Bud. "I was getting ready to call him, but then Chloe called and asked if I wanted to come out."

"She did?" I shot a look at Chloe, who waved a little wave.

And then there was Miles, suddenly standing next to me. He stuck his hand out for Kathryn to shake.

"I think I've seen you around school," he said. He nudged in closer, getting between Kathryn and me. "You're taking Trig or something like that, right?"

"Yes!" The gold in Kathryn's eyes flashed. "Your locker must be on the math wing. You're always there when I get out of class."

"Fascinating," said Miles. "Now why didn't I notice you sooner?"

I stood there, staring at Miles's back, feeling the warm, happy feeling from just a few minutes ago drain away. I broke off and grabbed Chloe's arm.

"Well, hey there, Brooke," she chattered as I pulled her over to the fireplace. "Long time no see!"

"What are you doing?" I asked.

"What do you mean?" Her shoulders went up in a clueless shrug.

"You know what I mean. Calling Kathryn. Bringing her here."

"You're kidding, right?" Chloe put her hands on her hips. "The whole point of the rush party was making new friends. But we were supposed to share them, not go off and treat everybody else like they're lepers."

"I didn't treat you like you're a leper," I said, reaching for an excuse that was true enough to sound convincing. "We've been busy with music. You hate that kind of thing."

But Chloe isn't stupid. There was no way to pretend I hadn't been avoiding her for three weeks straight.

"So what are you saying, Brooke?" she said. "That Kathryn can only be your friend?"

"That's not what I meant."

"Then what *did* you mean?"

I looked over her shoulder to see Boodawg handing Kathryn a glass that looked like it had wine in it. To Chloe, Kathryn was just somebody new to talk about. A pledge for her little junior class sorority. I thought about trying to explain what Kathryn was to me, but I knew she would never understand.

"Just because I like her doesn't mean you have to make her into a project," I said.

"Kathryn isn't a *project*, Brooke. I'm trying to be nice." Chloe squinted at me. "What were *you* planning to do with her, hide her someplace and only let her come out when you say it's okay?"

"No . . . ," I said. Putting it like that made the whole thing seem shallow and stupid.

"I like her," Chloe went on. "Dina likes her. You obviously like her. There's no reason why we can't all hang out, right, Brooke?"

Okay. On the surface, she *was* right. Perfectly reasonable. And I had to agree, because keeping up the argument would only make me look stupid. But watching from across the room while Kathryn talked to Miles and Dina in that dress and those boots, I didn't feel reasonable at all. What I really felt was scared.

SENIOR YEAR

*Stretto: the overlapping of the same theme or motif by
two voices a few beats apart*

BROOKE

IT'S MONDAY. THE MONDAY AFTER the pool party, and everybody's wondering when Kathryn will come back to school. She stayed home Friday, which got the rumor mill going good. In just a couple days, the story has gone from a bloody lip and a bump on the head to a weekend at the hospital on life support. That one scared me when I first heard it. What if she really did get hurt? What if she got water in her lungs or went too long without air and had brain damage? I tell myself it can't be that bad. Anderson would have said something, and he hasn't mentioned Kathryn at all. What he did say, Friday at the end of choir, was that we'd be getting the repertoire for fall contests today.

Sure enough, when we walk in at the start of class there are black folders stacked on top of the piano. For a few minutes, they're what everybody's talking about. Until Kathryn walks in. People start whispering, looking for signs of a near-death experience. She doesn't look like she's had any major injuries, though. She keeps her eyes down and stays quiet. She doesn't look at me at all.

The folders are stacked by section. I take mine back to my seat and flip through it. Brahms, Bach, a couple of contemporary pieces. Anderson waits until everybody's got one, then he steps up to his music stand.

"Let's begin with the Vivaldi."

We sight-read the first couple of pages. When a new movement starts, my eyes go down to the second staff, looking for the alto part. There's nothing there. I look at the soprano staff. The notes go on all by themselves across the top of the page. Right above the time signature is the word "solo."

"Kathryn," says Anderson. "Go ahead and take this."

I flip ahead in the music. Nothing there, so I search through the rest of my folder, looking for my piece. If Kathryn gets a solo, Anderson always evens it out by giving me one, too. It's like this unspoken balance he's set up. Like he knows about this thing between us and wants everything to be fair.

But this time it isn't.

Maybe he feels bad about what happened at the pool. Maybe Kathryn got to him somehow—told him she wanted a solo and got him to agree. Or maybe he thinks Kathryn is better than me.

It can't be that. It better not be. Kathryn starts to sing and the sound of her voice is terrifying. She obviously spent all summer practicing. A few chairs over, Laura Lindner rolls her eyes at me. Normally I'd be all over anything that knocks Kathryn off her precious little pedestal, but today she sounds way too good.

Kathryn's always been a threat but now, with the Blackmore coming up, she just might be my biggest competition.

Two hours later when school lets out, I'm still obsessing about it. I want to go home and practice, but Chloe's waiting by my locker. Her normally perfect makeup looks faded, and her eyes are bloodshot.

"Have you been crying?" I ask.

"No." She presses her cheeks with her fingertips. "It's just allergies. You're the one who looks like crap."

"Gee, thanks," I say, and start on my locker combination.

"So," she says through a stopped-up nose. "What's the matter?"

I take a breath. Maybe if I say it, then I'll feel better. "Kathryn."

Chloe scrunches up her face. "Kathryn who? Kathryn Pease?"

I nod, and Chloe's expression gets darker.

"What about her?"

"Kathryn is . . ." This is music related, so I know I'll have to ease Chloe into it. "Kathryn is driving me crazy."

"But I thought we took care of her last year."

"We did," I say, remembering. "I mean, *I* did."

"Right. So what's the problem?"

I try again. This time with a little more detail. "You can talk all you want about 'taking care of her.' But that didn't make her disappear. She's a good singer."

"Exactly my point." Chloe throws her hands up. "She's a music freak."

"She got a solo today in choir and I didn't."

"Devastating, Brooke. Really."

"It sort of is."

I slam my locker door. Harder than I need to, but Chloe doesn't seem to notice. "Forget about Kathryn," she tells me. "Right now you've got bigger things to worry about."

"Oh yeah?" I say. "Like what?"

"Like this."

She pulls a sheet of paper out of her bag and hands it to me. It's the Spirit Committee's list of Homecoming court nominees. "Nobody's supposed to see it until tomorrow. Don't say I never do anything for you."

I read all of the names. Mine is first on a list with four other girls. Angela Van Zant, Kiersten Coons, Celina DeGraff, Madison Verbeck . . .

"You're not on here," I say.

"Of course I'm not. I'm organizing the whole thing, so it would be a total conflict of interest for me to be a candidate, too."

I look into her eyes, which are definitely red. She coughs and rubs her nose.

"Are you sure you're okay with this?" Chloe's been dying to be in the Homecoming court ever since junior high, when Brice and Bill would take us to high school football games. Afterward, she would dress up in my mom's old cabaret gowns and practice blowing kisses to my stuffed animals.

"I wouldn't say it if I didn't mean it," she tells me. "Besides, you need me, Brooke. Without my help you'd squander an opportunity like this."

She looks so serious that I have to laugh. "Was 'squander' on one of your vocab tests this week?"

"Indubitably. Now give me that before anybody else sees it." She takes the list back, but not before I check out the guys. I find John Moorehouse's name, third down.

"So," Chloe says. "Have you thought about your campaign?"

"Please," I groan. "You're not serious."

"I'm dead serious. See, Brooke? This is why you need me so much."

"But campaign? Even you said it was stupid." A few years ago, the school board decided the Spirit Committee needed to do more than just organize parties and pep rallies. So they came up with this thing where the people nominated for Homecoming court have to pick some kind of cause they want to represent. When everybody goes to vote, they pay a dollar. However many votes you get, that's how much money goes to your cause. It sounds good in theory, but only about half the people in our school actually vote. With ten people on the court, the most anybody ever raises is a couple hundred dollars.

"It's not stupid, Brooke," Chloe tells me. "With me as your campaign manager, you're going to make the most money of anybody." She's actually rubbing her hands together, like a little Ivanka Trump. "So what's your cause?"

"Well." I think a minute. "I'm for sure not doing something sappy like the stray-cat shelter."

Then it hits me. Honors Choir. Our dresses are expensive. Nobody helps us buy them, even though the football players get their uniforms for free. Maybe I can start a fund to help buy dresses for the girls who can't afford them.

"You want to put choir dresses on your campaign posters," Chloe says when I tell her. "Really."

"Hey, it's my choice what I raise money for. I'm responding to a real need." Chloe's resistance makes me even more determined. "It's choir dresses or nothing. I never asked to go up for Homecoming Queen."

She sighs. "Fine. We'll just have to come up with a sexy slogan." Without asking if I've got anything better to do, she grabs my hand and drags me clear across the building to the art wing. Hidden in one of the back studios are sheets of bright-colored poster board. Chloe opens up a locker and starts pulling out Magic Markers, glitter, and glue.

"When did you get all this?" I say.

"Yesterday." Paint. Stickers. She must've cleaned out the entire crafts store. "But I'm not doing anything else unless you help me, got it? God, Brooke, if everybody loved me as much as they love you, I wouldn't be so freaking blasé about it." She shoves a can of spray paint into my hand. I hesitate. I really do need to get home and practice. But Chloe's already made up some slogans, so I get to work, helping her paint them onto the posters. The art studio has big doors that open off the back of the building. They're standing wide-open, and a nice breeze comes through. Football practice is going on. I can hear a whistle and yelling outside.

But the open doors don't do much to get rid of the paint fumes.

"I'm about to keel over," I tell Chloe. "I'm going for some air."

Outside, I pace around the bottom of the little hill that leads up to the stadium. A whistle blows break time and the guys start coming down to the trainer's truck for drinks. They all say hi as they walk past me.

And there's John Moorehouse, bringing up the back.

Okay. I should be used to seeing John by now. But I can't help it—every time he comes near me I get all hot and my brain goes fizzy-blank.

"Hey, Brooke."

Oh my God. He's stopping.

"How're the twins?"

His hair is wet and sticking up all over from being inside his helmet. There are black smudges underneath his eyes. These days I'm pretty snarky when people ask about Bill and Brice, but this is John Moorehouse. He could ask me pretty much anything.

"They're okay," I say. "They were home over the weekend. They start school tomorrow."

"I thought they'd be at The Rocks on Saturday. I didn't see you there, either."

"I had to practice." I say it before I can catch myself. I wait for his eyes to glaze over, like everybody else's do when the topic of music comes up.

But instead he says, "You're doing that contest, right?

The Blackmore Festival?"

My jaw almost hits the ground. "*You* know about the Blackmore?"

"My dad's firm is a big sponsor. But all I've been hearing is how it might not happen since the new hall's so far behind schedule."

I've heard that rumor, too. The new Buxton-Blackmore recital hall was supposed to be part of the festival's big fiftieth anniversary celebration, but it's turned into a big drama instead. Every time I go to Baldwin for my voice lessons I check on how the construction is going. It never seems much further along, even though the crews are supposedly working on it 24/7.

"The application said November fifteenth," I tell John. "And it better be on because I'm totally doing it."

"I bet you'll be amazing." He punches my arm. I put my hand over the spot and try not to look embarrassed. "What's that on your face?"

"What?" I look for my reflection in one of the glass doors. There's a dark streak across my nose. I can't tell if it's red or black. "Um . . . ," I say, licking my finger and rubbing at it, "it's either marker or paint. We're making Homecoming posters in the art room."

"I thought we weren't finding out the court until tomorrow."

"Well . . ." I think about Chloe and the art supplies

that just happened to be all ready and waiting in her locker. "Chloe can't keep a secret."

"Surprise, surprise."

"But now that I know . . ." I shouldn't be doing this, but it will keep him here longer. And I like having something he can't get anywhere else.

"Yeah?" He leans in.

"You're on the list, too."

"Aw, really?" He looks pumped. "We could be King and Queen together!"

"We could!" Suddenly the idea of campaigning doesn't seem like such a bad thing.

The coach blows his whistle. The break is over.

"Whoops!" says John. "I forgot my drink!"

"You wasted your break!" Now I'm totally flirting. It's obnoxious, but John doesn't seem to mind.

"I wouldn't exactly call it wasted," he says. When he smiles, his eyes crinkle under the smudgepaint. I watch him grab some Gatorade from the back of the pickup; then he runs back up the hill, his rear end looking completely distracting in those tight uniform pants.

Hot *and* knowledgeable about all-important singing contests—could one guy get any more perfect?

Chloe's shaking a new can of paint when I get back inside.

"Who were you talking to?" she asks.

"Nobody," I say. Fortunately, she's too busy painting to nag, so I pick up a can and start spraying, too.

We spend three more hours on the posters, and it's almost seven when I finally get home. There's a frozen TV dinner melting on the kitchen counter with a note from my mom stuck on top.

Strategy meeting tonight. Sorry I missed you. Your father called. He's at the apartment in NYC.

I dig in my purse for my cell phone. Yep, he's texted me.

New Project: SanFran Opera. Money factor: 7. Cool factor: 10. Call soon.

John Moorehouse talked to me.

My dad called.

I feel much better now.

I put the dinner back in the freezer and take a banana up to my bedroom. I try calling Dad three times but can't get him on the phone, so I text him congratulations. Then I wander over to my piano. On a day with no Homecoming posters to make, I would have been done practicing by now. I try to do at least an hour every day. I have ever since I was a kid, singing for my dad in front of all his friends.

Back when my parents were together, they used to have these great parties. Every weekend, our apartment would be filled with people—actors, artists, people from Mom's cabaret or whatever show Dad happened to be working on. At some point in the evening, somebody would always sit down at the piano and my mom would do a couple of songs.

One night, Dad got me in on the act. He'd caught me earlier in the day, singing along with my mom's CDs. That night, he grabbed me out of the crowd and stood me up next to the piano.

"Brookie does the best Ella Fitzgerald you've ever seen!" he announced. "Go on, honey. Do 'Cottontail,' just like today."

I turned away and stuck my finger in my mouth. I was terrified.

"Don't be shy," Dad said. "Show them what you can do."

He turned me back around and knelt in front of me with this big smile on his face. I couldn't let him down. So I started singing, extraloud. I even made up some dance steps. When I finished, the whole room exploded with applause.

"That's my girl!" Dad said. He picked me up and put a big kiss on my cheek.

After that, my singing was a Dempsey party tradition. Right before my bedtime, people would gather around the piano and make tinkling noises on their wineglasses. That was my cue. Dad would smile proudly while I sang show tunes or jazz classics. When I got older he started taking me to operas, and then I'd do easier versions of the arias we saw at Wolf Trap or Lincoln Center. When it was over, he would lift me up on his shoulders and carry me around so everybody could tell me what a great job I'd done.

"That's my girl," he always said. "My Little Star."

The piano is upstairs now, in my studio. On the back of it there's a picture of me and my dad. I'm wearing a dirndl and yellow braids from a *Sound of Music* parody my mom wrote. Dad's wearing a red sweater. He's holding me tight, smashing my cheek into his chin. I look at the picture as I begin my warm-up, remembering how stubby his beard felt. How much I loved it when he hugged me like that. Instead of practicing the songs for my next lesson, I reach into the piano bench and pull out a book of old Sondheim songs. I can hear Dad's voice as I start to sing through them. It's almost enough to drown out thoughts about Kathryn. Let her have the solo in choir. Let her be beautiful and tiny and all of the things I'm not. It doesn't matter because I'm going to go to Homecoming with John Moorehouse. And then, I'm going to win the Blackmore.

I can just hear Dad now. He'll come backstage and put his arms around me. "My Little Star," he'll say. Then he'll take me back to New York, and I'll start a whole new life—the one I was supposed to have all along.

KATHRYN

"IT'S GOOD," I TELL MATT. He holds my arm and steers me through the morning hallway traffic while I read his first piece for the *Douglas Picayune*. Launching the "Geek God" column was my first order of business when I took the job of features editor; since Matt barely passes English every year, I figured it would help him focus if he could write about topics that really interest him.

"You don't think it sucks?" He maneuvers me away from a teacher pushing an A/V cart while I use my red pen to delete a couple of errant commas.

"Not at all. You actually make fan fiction sound cool. Just watch—the A-listers will be reading slash by the end of the week."

"It is my goal in life to get the cheerleaders hot over some Jack/Sawyer action. Or Harry/Ron." He chuckles. "I always thought Dina Mendoza seemed like a closet

Potterslash fan."

"Genius." I hand him back his paper and let my eyes readjust to the path ahead of me. "So what's your next one going to be about? Cosplay? RPGs?"

"I thought I'd focus closer to home. Talk about people who live out their passions IRL. Like you and how you're getting ready to do the Blackmore on top of the paper and choir and everything else."

I shake my head, suddenly uncomfortable. "Nobody wants to read about me."

"But you're the big soloist!"

"Actually, I think I'm going to turn that down. Regionals are for large ensembles, not solos. And the only people who really care about the Blackmore are the other singers."

"More people care about the Blackmore than care about fanfic," he says. "Methinks there's a bigger reason you're shunning the spotlight."

Before I can stop him he's grabbed my backpack and thrust his hand inside.

"I knew it!" He snatches out the yellow Blackmore entry and holds it over his head. "You haven't sent it in yet!"

"No." I blush. "Because if you must know, I'm thinking maybe I won't do the Blackmore. I have too much going on anyway with school and stuff, plus I applied for a lot of scholarships. I'm sure one of those will come through, and then I won't have to be distracted from my schoolwork by getting ready for a music competition."

I stand on tiptoe and grab the entry form away. Matt lets it slide from his fingers, humming softly. I groan. "Not the bushel song again."

He bumps me with his shoulder and pseudoshouts, "No!" I'm about to smack him with the yellow envelope when he says, "Hey, what's that?"

Up ahead, near the big double doors leading to the front courtyard, a poster is taped to the wall. As we get closer, I can see the word "Dempsey" in big red letters. A few feet away, on the same wall, is a piece of white paper with two rows of names on it.

"Homecoming nominations," Matt says. "They must've just posted them."

We go over to look at the list, and then I look closer at Brooke's campaign poster. DRESS A NEEDY CHOIRGIRL, it says, above a line about how she wants to raise money for people who can't afford their Honors Choir gowns.

"Oh my God."

"What's wrong?" Matt says.

I point to the bit about the dresses, and Matt reads more closely.

"So?"

"What do you mean, so? Last week she tries to drown

me and now this? This is tailor-made to freak me out."

He shakes his head. "But why now? She hasn't done anything this blatant in months."

I hold up the yellow application. "This is why. The Blackmore is less than three months away. It's the one place where she can't just say the word and smack me down."

I look around for other campaign posters and see none. There's only one way to explain how Brooke was able to get hers out so early: She must have known in advance that she was nominated; it's just the kind of thing her friends would do for her, and it's not fair to anybody else, but nobody will say anything about it. They never do. Brooke is the kind of girl people make exceptions for.

The warning bell rings. Matt offers to walk me to Anatomy, but I tell him no, I'm fine.

"Are you sure?" he asks.

"Yes," I lie. "You're going to be late for Chem."

He squeezes my shoulder, and then he's off. I, on the other hand, am stuck in front of Brooke's sign, fighting feelings I thought I'd conquered months ago: anger, dread, and a trapped sort of sensation that is worse than the incident at Brooke's pool, because it's clear now that this is just the beginning. I haven't even turned in my registration and the competition has already started.

All around me, people are rushing to class. I tear myself away and follow, trying to fight back the suspicion that they're all staring at me, just like they did after Homecoming last year.

Outside of the Anatomy lab, a cheerleader pinches her nose. "Oh, gross!" she says to her friend. "Smell that!"

I pull my arms in close; of course I assume they're talking about me. But then I smell it, too—an odor like wet rubber and rancid syrup. It's coming from inside the lab. I step into the classroom and find the source: Every other table holds a pallet on which rests the ghostly pale body of a fetal pig. I never thought I'd be grateful to see dead animals, but I am beyond happy that there really is a smell, and it's coming from them.

Ms. Burke, our new science teacher, claps her hands as the last bell rings.

"All right, everyone," she calls. "There aren't enough specimens to go around, so partner up. You'll be using the same one all semester, so don't start cutting until you've studied the directions carefully."

I watch as people start to pair off, dreading the idea of having to ask someone to work with me. I'm working up the nerve to approach a new guy sitting in the back row when a voice comes over my shoulder.

"I used to hunt wild hogs back in Iowa. If you cook 'em just right, they make a good pork roast."

I look up, into a pair of green eyes belonging to John Moorehouse, a transfer from last spring and probably the most amazing-looking guy at school.

I stand frozen, trying not to appear surprised.

"I guess what I'm trying to say," he continues, "is if you need someone to help you butcher little Porky, then I'm your man."

In the movies that Matt and I watch there's always a star football player, the guy who all the others look up to and the girls want to end up with. John is like that. I've seen him in the halls but never thought much about him—mostly because he's an A-lister, which means he's part of Brooke's world.

"We don't have to be partners," he says. "I can ask somebody else."

"No," I say, forcing myself to snap out of it. "That's okay. I mean, we can work together. If you want to."

"Great." He smiles. Then he motions for me to join him at a table by the window, where an unclaimed pig lies, looking pearly and almost translucent from the preserving fluid. After listening to Ms. Burke lecture about the proper way to begin the dissection, we get out scissors and scalpels and, following the diagrams she's posted at the front of the room, we start cutting into the pig. It isn't as disgusting as I'd thought it would be; the most disturbing thing is the odor. It sticks in your nostrils and makes everything smell chemically sweet.

After we've made the initial incisions, we have a lot of delicate work to do separating the connective tissue that holds the skin to the muscles. John starts slicing through the filmy white tissue, concentrating hard.

"I just saw the Homecoming nominations," I say. "You're up for King. Congratulations."

"Thanks." John checks Ms. Burke's PowerPoint, then starts to tackle the area around the pig's thigh. "It's not that big a deal, though."

"It is to everybody else," I tell him. "Homecoming is huge here at Douglas."

He smiles. "Well, then it's huge to me, too, I guess. At least as far as football goes. But the King stuff? Not so much."

"I would think you'd like getting picked out of the crowd like that. It means people like you."

"All it really means is that they get to see me make a fool out of myself in a stupid cape and crown."

I giggle at the image. "Now I hope you win it."

"You'd better not be laughing like that if I do." His voice sounds serious even though his words are a joke. "Who are you going with, anyway?"

"I don't know." I hadn't planned on going to Homecoming at all, but I don't want John to think I'm a loser, so I tell him I'll probably go with Matt.

"Is Matt your boyfriend?"

I stop, my scalpel hovering. This isn't the first time I've been asked the question, and I guess I'd be lying if I said I never thought about it; in those old movies, the best guy friend usually ends up having feelings for the heroine. But every time I do think about it, the idea of changing what we are—what we've been for so long—is just too much.

"It's purely platonic," I tell John.

He nods. "I wonder if Matt would say the same thing." The bell starts to ring, and he pulls a piece of plastic over the pig. "Well, that's that. See you tomorrow?"

"Tomorrow," I murmur. "Okay . . ."

He stacks our pallet on a tall metal cart, along with the pigs belonging to the others in our class, and then, before I can say anything else, he is out of the room.

For the rest of the day I can't get his comment out of my mind. *Would* Matt say the same thing? How ridiculous—of course he would. Mixed up in the muddle is the memory of the way John smiled when he asked me to be his partner. Driving home, I replay the encounter, trying to decipher every nuance.

Is Matt your boyfriend?

When I pull into my driveway, my mother is sitting alone on the front porch. She waves as I'm parking, and when I start up the walk I can see that she has a stack of papers in her lap.

"These came in the mail today," she says, fanning them out hopefully. I see the college crests on the envelopes and walk slower; I had no idea they'd be getting back to me so quickly.

I drag myself up the steps and sit beside her.

"How was school?" she asks. She wears the khakis and white polo shirt that go under her work smock; a glint of gray threads through her thick, dark hair.

Brooke, the Homecoming poster, John . . . if I were to try and tell her everything we would be out on the steps all evening, so I just say, "Busy. Those came back fast."

"Yes." She pushes the envelopes into my hands. "I don't know if that's a good or bad thing. I guess we'll find out, right?"

There are three of them. First I open the one for the school I sent writing samples to. . . . . *A surplus of outstanding candidates . . . limited funds . . .* I didn't get the scholarship.

"It's okay." Mom smoothes the front of her shirt. "It's only the first one."

The other two are for music programs, and I feel better about my chances there. Both of the letters are good news—just not enough.

"Fifteen hundred a semester," says Mom, reading over my shoulder. "What's the tuition?"

"Ten thousand a year."

Her face drops. "What does the other letter say?"

"Three thousand plus free housing in the honors hall for musicians." She brightens again, until I tell her that tuition at that school is even more than at the first one.

She gathers up the papers, stacking them neatly because I know she's thinking we shouldn't trash an offer of money, no matter how puny it is.

"It's only the first three," she says. "These aren't even very prestigious schools, and they obviously don't know what they're doing if they can't reward talent like yours."

"I'm not worried," I tell her as I get to my feet, although inside I've started to get that trapped feeling again—the sensation of something unseen and ominous bearing down on me. "Something will come through."

"Of course it will," she answers. "With your grades and your voice, how could it not?"

I can think of dozens of ways it could not, actually. All this time I've been afraid that the scary something at the end of the tunnel was a competition, but now I see that competing might just be my only way out. Winning means escaping the pressure of standing apart from thousands of other scholarship seekers. Winning means going to college without having to drain my parents' bank account.

It also means getting back at Brooke. She may be the

Queen B, but I'm the one who got a solo in choir. I'm also the one who really needs the money.

This needy choirgirl is about to shine.

Mom and I go inside, she to the kitchen and me to the guest room upstairs, where the computer waits with its screen saver of musical notes marching across a bloodred background. I take the Blackmore letter from my backpack, wake up the computer, and call up the special link for competitors. I fill out the registration form quickly, stopping only when I get to the part where they request payment information, and then I call Matt.

"You can't see the Matt Melter™ over the phone," I say. "But I have a favor to ask that will put me forever in your debt."

"Forever is a long time," he replies. "But the Matt Melter™ is powerful. So shoot."

I take a deep breath, grab a Post-it, and uncap my ink pen.

"Remember how you told me I could borrow your credit card number for the Blackmore? Well, I'm ready. What is it?"

BROOKE

I CAN'T REACH DAD.

First I try the apartment in New York. Nobody answers. So I call L.A. No answer there, either. He must have started the San Francisco job already. I dial up his cell phone. It rings and rings. Finally, I leave a message on voice mail: "Hey, Daddy, it's Brooke. Could you call me as soon as you can? I've got that big contest coming up. The Blackmore. It's November fifteenth, and I need some help. You can call me back anytime you want. I'll be up late."

I practice for an hour, then add on another half just to give him time to call back. The phone stays quiet. I check the ringer: on. Texts? None. Just to be safe, I open my laptop. His name doesn't show up on my IM screen, so I get myself some water to sip while I write him an email. It ends up being longer than I'd planned. I go back through and delete more than half. I'll tell him all the details when we talk.

Then I wait. For more than fourteen hours.

"Hey, Brooke."

A plate of pad thai comes into focus in front of me. Somehow I managed to sleepwalk through the entire next morning at school, plus the walk to the Chinese restaurant where everybody hangs out over lunch. I have a vague memory of Chloe jabbering about Homecoming. But I must have lost track somewhere between "parade floats" and "spa treatments for the entire court."

I shove some cold, rubbery noodles into my mouth, trying not to elbow Dina in the process. Our table is packed and she's pretty much sitting right on top of me while Chloe's knees play bumper cars with mine from across the table.

"I'm eating," I say to Chloe. It's an all-purpose response that's supposed to buy time while I figure out what topic we're on now. But Chloe just looks at me weird.

"I didn't say anything," she says. "It was your visitor here."

She points over my shoulder and I turn to see Laura Lindner standing there, hugging her purse and looking nervous as hell.

"Hey, Brooke," Laura repeats.

"Hey . . ." I swallow and stare. I have no idea what she's doing here. She looks like she's still figuring it out, too.

"So I've never been to this place," Laura says with a choked-sounding laugh. "Which is weird since it's so close to school. Everybody says such great things about the food, though. I thought I'd give it a try. . . ."

I decide to put her out of her misery. Everybody knows the food here sucks.

"Do you want to sit with us?"

"Really?" She hugs her purse tighter. A few feet over, John Moorehouse slides up a chair along with Bud Dawes and two other football players. He catches my eye and waves. Laura looks like she's about to pee her pants. Meanwhile Chloe is squinting at me over her Diet Coke like, *What the hell?*

"Hey, Chlo," I say. "This is Laura. We're in choir together."

"You and I were in the same Spanish class last year," Laura tells Chloe. "We did that skit about ordering dinner at the world's worst restaurant? Tim McNamara pretended like he was throwing up and dumped a jar of salsa all over the table."

"Oh right." Chloe stirs her drink with her straw and smiles. "I knew you reminded me of something."

"And how flattering," adds Dina. "It's vomit."

The whole table goes quiet. Laura's smile starts to wobble, and I feel Chloe kick Dina under the table. "Don't mind Dina," Chloe says. "She's a little bit challenged in the good manners department."

"Don't you want to get your food?" I ask.

And I have to hand it to Laura, she recovers quick. "Right!" she says, smiling full-on again. "Be right back."

Laura hurries over to the food counter. Chloe looks over at Dina, and they both start giggling. "Oh dear . . . ," says Chloe, as if what just happened is the most tragic thing she's ever seen.

"Don't," I tell her.

"What?" she says.

"Seriously," I hiss. I glance around the table at Dina, Angela, Jenna, and Madison, and I whisper, "Be nice."

"Oh whatever, Brooke. I'm not going to bite her."

When Laura returns to the table with a plate of fried rice, we scoot our chairs over to make room. Then Chloe turns with a fascinated expression that manages to look almost genuine.

"So! Laura! You've got to tell us: Who's hot and who's not over in the music wing?"

On our way back to school, John catches up with me.

"I saw your Homecoming posters," he says. "Dress a needy choirgirl. That's a good one."

"Thanks." My heart starts thudding, so hard I'm afraid I'll puke up my pad thai. "I actually thought it up myself."

I walk a little straighter, peeking around to see if anybody is looking. But Chloe and Dina and Laura are up ahead, and Laura's giving Chloe a run for her money in the marathon talking department.

As we get up to the building, we can hear the first bell ringing. John runs to the door and holds it open for me. Inside, the hallway is crowded so we have to press in close. Even though we're pushing it on time, I slow down and switch my backpack to my other shoulder so he can get even closer.

"Where you headed?" he asks.

"Choir."

"Mind if I walk you?"

This is it! I shake my head. My heart does an extra-hard thump.

"So I wanted to ask you something."

I was right. He's going to ask me to Homecoming. But the final bell is ringing. And as we turn into the music wing, I see the door to the choir room shut. Crap. Anderson hates it when people are late.

And *I* am hating myself right now. If I weren't so paranoid about what my choir director thinks, I'd be savoring every detail of this moment. I stop walking and turn my back to the door.

There. I can focus now.

"What's up?"

"I'm trying for a football scholarship at U of M," he says. "Going up there in a month, and I needed someplace to stay. Do you think Bill and Brice would let me shack up with them for a day or two?"

"Um . . . ," I say while my brain rushes to process the disconnect between what I thought he was going to say and what he's actually said. *Crap,* goes the little voice inside my brain.

But then another little voice tells me maybe it's not that bad. It isn't very romantic asking somebody to Homecoming when you're rushing to get to class on time. John's probably waiting for a more private opportunity.

"I don't think they'll care," I say. "I'll call tonight and ask."

"Great," he says, flashing those amazing green eyes. "We'll talk later?"

"Yeah," I tell him. "Later."

He takes off and I rush into the choir room. "Nice of you to join us, Brooke," Anderson shouts while I run up the risers to my spot.

I take a second to get myself into singing mode. Try to forget about John and concentrate on my voice. I open my mouth for the first scale and nothing comes out. I clear my throat. Try again. Better, but it's still hard to get any volume. I must be getting hoarse.

Great.

Kathryn, on the other hand, sounds really good. And suddenly I've got a whole new reason to be pissed at myself. What am I doing worrying about Homecoming when I should be focusing on the Blackmore? I've got to quit wasting energy on things that don't matter and practice more. After everything that's happened between us, I can't let Kathryn win. If I have to watch somebody else take first place, I could almost stand it. Almost. As long as that other person isn't her.

JUNIOR YEAR

Minaccioso: to take on an increasingly threatening or ominous tone

KATHRYN

BEFORE JUNIOR YEAR, I ALWAYS assumed that the Cinderella stories were a fantasy. Nobody in the real world ever woke up one morning to find themselves part of the most powerful crowd at school. The fabulous people were born to their fabulous lives; mousy nobodies like me had their place, and though the two worlds might sometimes overlap, crossing over was pretty much impossible.

Yet that's what I'd managed to do, and it didn't take a magic spell or even much of an effort on my part; all it took was one night at Bud Dawes's house. Before Bud's party, it was as if I only really existed as a shadow, visible to a handful of people. Then Chloe and Dina turned on a light and suddenly everyone could see me; most amazing of all was that they seemed to like what they saw. People started saying hello to me in the hallways and in class, and I had friends—more than

I'd ever had before.

I also had a boyfriend—sort of.

"Lucky girl," purred Dina as we watched Miles Monaghan's backside move away from us across the commons. The ten-minute break between second and third hour had just started, and Miles had grabbed me as I headed to my locker after Intermediate French. Dina and Chloe came up just as he was asking me to the movies for Saturday.

"Ugh, you're *so* lucky," said Chloe. She motioned for me to sit next to her on the bench that, I now knew, was reserved for A-listers. "And I happen to know Miles is on the Senior Keg organizing team. Do you think you could get us an invite?"

I couldn't believe it; was Chloe Romelli really asking *me* for social favors? Miles and I had been dating for two weeks, ever since the party, and I'd found that seeing him definitely had its perks. He was handsome and smart, plus he treated me like I was the only person in the room. The only problem was that he also had a habit of treating other people like *they* were the only ones in the room, right in front of me. During our first date, a beautiful Asian girl came up behind him in the restaurant and rested her hands on his shoulders. He put his hands over hers and pulled her toward our table so that her cheek came to rest against his.

"Mei," he murmured. "Where have you been? You don't call me anymore."

The girl gave me the kind of glance I imagined one would give the eight-year-old child of a parent's coworker. "Fall break, silly," she replied. "I've been in Maryland. Plus, you know, I have a life."

Miles tugged on one of the girl's arms, coaxing her around so that she had to crouch beside him. "Don't disappear like that again," he said, gazing deep into her eyes. "You'll break my heart."

"I'd worry about it," she said, "if I thought you actually had a heart." And then she slinked back to a table of sophisticated-looking older girls.

"That was Mei," Miles told me as he tucked back into his pasta. "She's a first-year at Baldwin. I met her at the park. We were both feeding the ducks."

"She looks . . ." I searched for the appropriate word. "Nice."

He nodded, leaned across the table, and fixed me with one of his *it's only you and me here* gazes. "She *is* nice," he said. "She's pretty incredible, actually."

So were we together, or were we just going on a few dates? I needed to talk about it with somebody, but Brooke had been getting to choir late and ducking out early so we couldn't talk, and rushing off the phone with a "sorry, gotta go," whenever I called. When I tried to catch up with her after school she was always holed up in a practice room until, finally, I gave up and went home by myself.

Matt, meanwhile, told me point-blank that he wouldn't be giving advice. "Miles Monaghan is a player," he'd said. "If you want to mess with a guy like that, you're on your own."

That didn't stop him from checking up on me, though.

"Don't look now," Chloe said after Miles had been swallowed up by the midmorning crush. "I think you're being stalked."

I turned to see what she meant and there was Matt, standing across the commons, watching us. I motioned for him to come over; he shook his head.

"That's Matt McWalter," I said. "You should meet him."

Dina wrinkled her nose. "I think I know him. He's in my Civics class."

"Right!" I said. "He's got Civics fourth period."

"He's a total geek. Seriously. One time he went off on this whole long rant about how the United States is like that eyeball guy from *Lord of the Rings* and how all the oppressed people are going to rise up and take away our power someday."

I cringed, able to imagine just what Matt had sounded like. I prayed he hadn't spoken Elvish in front of Dina.

"Lord of the Rings?" laughed Chloe. "Somebody actually *likes Lord of the Rings*? I only sat through it for the hot guys." My confidence started to crumble as she peered closer at Matt, as if studying a strange mole on somebody's skin. "Are you guys friends?" she said. "Really?"

"No." My cheeks burned; it was awful but I didn't want Chloe to think I was weird, too. "We're not *friends* friends. We live in the same neighborhood. Our parents used to make us play together. That's all."

Matt appeared to change his mind just then, deciding he would come over after all. As he started toward us, Chloe closed her fingers around my arm, and with one smooth, amazingly discreet motion, she pulled me off the bench and whisked me away down the hall.

"Don't take this the wrong way," she said, "but I think you've outgrown the Hobbit."

I looked back over my shoulder as we went around the corner, just in time to see Matt standing in the middle of the commons, alone.

That night I went to his house, bringing my mother's famous black forest brownies as a peace offering, and instead of sharing the frosting like we usually would, we had what felt oddly like a breakup.

"I get it," he told me as he put the plate of uneaten

sweets into the refrigerator. "I don't like it, but I get it."

"Are you all right?" I asked.

"Not really. But . . . do you want the truth here?"

"Of course," I replied.

"I could have told you it would end up like this. I pretty much saw it coming the first time you ever mentioned Brooke Dempsey to me."

Brooke. Her friendship was the spark for everything that had happened, yet I saw less and less of her as the days went by. On Friday, Miles didn't meet me in the commons, and when I tracked him down at lunch to ask whether he'd been able to get Chloe and Dina on the Senior Keg guest list, he told me he'd have to call me about it in the kind of voice that lets a person know their plans might be falling through. Suddenly, I felt unsure of everything. So I planted myself outside of Brooke's locker after school.

Five minutes stretched into fifteen before I finally saw her. She saw me, too, and for a split second it looked as if she was considering going the other direction.

"Hey," I said when she finally walked up and started her combination. "What are you doing?"

"Opening my locker," she replied, twisting the dial so violently that it spun past her target and she had to begin again.

"I mean what are you doing today?" I pressed. "After

129

you open your locker?"

"Going home to practice. I'm late for my ride."

"Do you want to go for coffee instead?"

"Don't you have plans with Miles?"

I let out a sharp breath; the sting of his brush-off was still fresh.

"I'm not with Miles," I told her. "At least I don't think I am."

She didn't answer. She tossed a notebook into her locker and pulled out her jacket, scanning the hallway as she put it on.

"Besides," I went on, "we're supposed to memorize that Poulenc piece for State. I thought we could do it together."

To my relief, she softened when I brought up music. "I heard you screw it up today," she said. "Anderson'll kill you if you do it again."

"See, I'm admitting I need help. Help!" I clasped my hands together and worked my face into a desperate frown.

She slammed her locker door shut. "Fine. We'll work on it at my place."

Brooke's house was cold and still when we arrived, just like it always was when I went over there. Even though I'd been home with her dozens of times, I still found the place amazing, with the foyer so big it actually echoed and the rooms filled with antiques and fine art. As we went up the front staircase to her room, I peered over the banister to see her brother Bill grab a basket of mail off the foyer table.

"Anything good?" Brooke shouted down to him.

"Doesn't look like it," he shouted back.

We were sitting side by side at her piano, working out Poulenc's difficult rhythms, when he snuck in behind us to drop an envelope onto the music stand. It was addressed to Brooke.

"When were you going to give this to me?" she said, snatching it up.

"It got stuck to the Beer of the Month Club catalog," Bill said. "Sue me."

She waited for him to leave before opening the envelope. "It's from my dad," she told me, and handed me the card inside. It was gorgeous, printed on handmade paper with a spare Japanese theme. Folded into it were snapshots of two men on a tropical beach.

"See, here he is," Brooke said, pointing to the taller man—the one who had her nose. The man standing next to him was suntanned with a big, toothy smile; I had the strange sense that I'd seen him someplace before.

"Wait a minute," I said. I remembered the movie Matt and I had rented a month earlier. "Is that . . . ?"

"Yeah," she replied.

"Your dad is with him? Really?"

"Yeah."

I looked more closely at the picture, at the crow's-feet around Jake Jaspers's eyes and the graying temples I'd never noticed in paparazzi shots. "I thought he was with Alexis McCoy."

"That's just an arrangement," said Brooke. "Alexis is a coke fiend and a kleptomaniac. She needs to keep her image clean, so she goes to premieres with Jake. His publicist is a real cobra. If reporters ask too many questions they get cut off from him *and* all the rest of her clients. So everybody just takes everything at face value. Jake and Alexis are together. Nobody says anything different, and everybody stays happy."

I thought about Matt, about what he would say if he knew. The movie we had rented was called *Mephistopheles*, and it starred Jake Jaspers as a futuristic fallen angel who could grant people's deepest wishes. Matt had liked it so much he'd raced online to get more information, a sure sign he was about to join a new fandom.

"Have you met him?" I asked.

"Of course," Brooke said. "Jake and Dad have been together for, like, ten years now."

"What's he like?"

"Totally different from how he acts in public. At premieres and stuff he's this big action hero type. When you see him in person he's this totally quiet househusband."

I squinted at the photograph, trying to picture it. "Does he ever come here—to Lake Champion?"

"Not much. Can you imagine?"

I couldn't. That Jake Jaspers had ever been in our town was unfathomable to me; that Brooke actually knew somebody like him was even more amazing. As if to prove her connection, she moved to her desk, opened a photo file on her laptop, and started clicking through the slide show. There were photos of Jake and her dad in London, photos of them relaxing in what appeared to be a posh apartment, photos of them looking like any other couple walking their dogs on a chilly Saturday in the park.

"Hm . . . ," I said as the images went by. "He looks heavier than in his movies."

"He uses a body double most of the time."

Another tropical picture came up. In this one, Jake Jaspers and her dad looked like they were standing at the edge of a giant volcano.

"Where are they now?" I asked.

"I think the Bahamas. Dad just closed a show, and they start shooting the *Mephistopheles* sequel in Romania next month. They wanted a break before they have to go out there."

"He didn't come visit you?"

"No."

"Do you miss him?"

"Yeah, but we talk all the time." She put her hand to the pendant around her neck, the one she never seemed to take off. "He used to call me his Little Star. Pretty stupid, huh?"

"No, it's sweet," I told her. "Your dad seems really cool."

She went back to the pictures, her face glowing in the light of the computer screen.

"Are you okay?" I asked.

"Yeah," she said, clicking. "It's funny, but I was going to say the same thing about your dad."

"You're kidding," I groaned. "My dad sits around the house doing Sudoku and updating his résumé. His biggest thrill is when I get my name in the paper for being on the honor roll. 'Cool' is the last word I would ever use to describe my dad."

The slide show of her father and Jake ended, giving way to images of Brooke and her friends from parties past. Click, click, click . . . the photos went by but Brooke stayed silent—for so long that I finally said, "Are you sure you're okay? Do you feel sick or something?"

"No," she murmured. "Maybe just a little lonely."

I let out a tiny laugh; I couldn't help it. "How can you

be lonely when so many people love you?"

She shrugged, and in the light of the screen I thought she looked sad, but I still didn't believe her. Sitting there in her big, beautiful house watching her beautiful life click by, I felt like I would gladly trade everything I had for just a fraction of what Brooke possessed—loneliness and all.

BROOKE

"READY, SET, GO!"

I dove into the pool, breaststroked across it and back, and then bobbed up near where Kathryn's feet were dangling in the water.

"A minute fifty-seven," she said. "Is that good?"

"Not good enough," I told her. "I need to shave off a couple more seconds before spring season starts. Time me again."

She gave the signal. I dove back into the water and came up doing a butterfly stroke. The exercise felt good. With nothing but the sound of splashing in my ears, I could finally think straight. Ever since Boodawg's party a few weeks earlier, this blackness had started creeping into how I felt about Kathryn. It was like somebody knocked over a can of paint the night Miles started acting all interested in her. The blackness started around the corners of everything, and it pushed in a little bit at a time. I tried to tell myself it wasn't her fault if Miles liked her. She didn't know I liked him, too. But knowing all that didn't help; I still had a hard time being around her.

Except when it was just Kathryn and me alone together. When the two of us could work on our music or hang out at the coffee shop and make plans about all the things we were going to do after leaving Douglas, then the blackness moved back and things felt almost like they did in the beginning.

Two laps. Up and back. I popped out of the water as Kathryn punched the stopwatch.

"A minute fifty-five seconds!" she said. "Good!"

She was sitting cross-legged on the pool deck in a tank top and cutoff shorts. Earlier, when I changed into my swimsuit, she'd told me she'd forgotten hers.

"You can get in with your clothes on," I told her. "Plenty of people have done it. It's no big deal."

"That's okay," she said. "I don't really feel like swimming."

"Why not? Afraid to get your hair wet?" I swam up and reached for her calves. She yanked back and stood up, looking freaked out.

"Don't do that."

"Um . . . okay." I pushed away from the side. "Sorry."

"I said I didn't feel like swimming."

"I know. I heard you. I said I was sorry."

She let her shoulders relax. After a couple of seconds, she came back to the edge of the pool and sat down.

"No, *I'm* sorry." She kept her feet under her legs and wouldn't put them back in the water. "I shouldn't freak out like that. It's just—God, this is embarrassing."

"What is?"

"I can't swim," she said, tugging on her ponytail. "I never learned how."

"How'd you manage to never learn? I thought everybody took swimming lessons when they were kids."

"I was always kind of afraid of water. And my mom and dad were spending so much on other things, like ballet and piano lessons, I guess they figured they'd save by not getting a Y membership. Only now I've got this phobia about pretty much anything deeper than a bathtub."

"Man, that sucks," I said. I thought about all the summers I'd spent at the pool as a kid—whole afternoons just floating by while my friends and I splashed around, getting waterlogged and tan. What had Kathryn been doing?

"Don't tell anybody, okay?" she said. "It's completely embarrassing."

She looked really vulnerable, which made me feel good in a weird kind of way. "No worries," I said. "You

can just keep on being my timekeeper."

She smiled and gripped the stopwatch. "Okay."

"Okay. So, ready? I still need to get rid of two seconds."

She reset the watch. Then she gave me the countdown. I dove in and tore through the water, faster than ever. I couldn't wait to get back to the other side and find out my time.

But when I popped up again, Kathryn wasn't there. I had to lift onto the deck to see where she went. First I saw her bare feet. And next to them, a pair of Ralph Lauren flip-flops.

"Crap . . . ," I muttered.

It was Chloe.

"Hey, Brooke," she called. "Kathryn said to come over."

The blackness started creeping in again as Chloe stripped off her T-shirt and jeans. She stretched, showing off her matching bra and panties and the little pearl in her perfect, pierced belly button. She dove into the pool with a big splash.

I got out. I didn't feel like swimming anymore.

Chloe came up for air. She backstroked around while Kathryn and I stood on the side.

"Hey, Kathryn!" Chloe shouted. "Get your clothes off and come in. I'm not swimming by myself."

Kathryn stopped smiling and blushed. "I'm okay. Really. You go ahead."

She looked trapped. And even though I was pissed at her for inviting Chloe over, I didn't want her to have to tell her secret to the biggest bigmouth in school. So I decided to try and help.

"We're quitting, actually," I said. "It's getting cold."

"What are you talking about? It's *not* cold. Seriously, Kath. Get in. What if it's your last chance until next year?"

"I don't have a suit."

"Hello?" Chloe pointed to her own pink bra, which by now was completely see-through. "Neither do I."

"I'm not skinny-dipping," Kathryn told her. "Sorry! No suit, no swim."

"So borrow one of Brooke's."

Then Kathryn did something weird. She started laughing.

"You're kidding, right? There's no way I'm fitting into something of Brooke's."

I felt like I'd been slapped in the face. It was true: Kathryn's probably a two to my size ten. But did she need to make a joke about it? She turned to me with a sorry little smile. I couldn't smile back. I was too busy trying to see through all of that black.

Chloe kept looking from me to Kathryn, then back to me again. She swam to the ladder and started to climb out. "Fine," she said. "God, Brooke. Talk about a buzzkill." I watched as Kathryn offered her my towel to dry off with. How did the whole thing get to be *my* fault?

I escaped to the kitchen for drinks and snacks, and when I came back outside, Chloe and Kathryn were in the gazebo, laughing their asses off.

"Oh my God, Brooke, you've got to hear this," said Chloe. "You know that guy Matt that Kathryn used to hang around with? He's into, like, Ren faires and stuff."

Kathryn looked like she expected me to laugh, too. But I didn't get the joke. Our junior high madrigal group performed at a Renaissance festival once. It was actually a lot of fun. I could see why Chloe wouldn't go for it. But Kathryn? I bet she'd been to a lot of Ren faires before, and liked them, too.

"He used to dress up in elf ears," Kathryn told us, stepping over and taking some lemonade from my tray. "And wear a cloak."

"No!" said Chloe.

"Yes!"

"Oh my GOD!"

"I know! Huzzah!" They both bent over, laughing so hard they almost spilled their drinks. I felt bad for Matt. He was the kind of person who kept to himself, but not in a snobbish way. More of an *I've got my own stuff going on* type of way. Everybody liked Matt—well, everybody who didn't have something to prove. But ever since Chloe started tagging along with me and Kathryn, I'd seen him lurking in the hallways with this lost look on his face. Kathryn never hung out with him anymore. When I asked her about it, she told me it was okay. "He gets it."

"Gets what?" I'd said.

"This," she'd replied, as if there was something about the two of us that made it impossible for her to have other friends. But the truth is that it wasn't just the two of us anymore. It was Chloe and Dina and Angela and all of the other people who grabbed and followed and acted like getting seen with us would make them part of some special group. It seemed like the days when Kathryn and I could hang out just the two of us were pretty much over.

I slumped in a chair and watched the two of them talking. I hated the way Kathryn wrinkled up her nose whenever Chloe made a joke. The way her eyes would get big, like every word Chloe said was the most interesting thing she'd ever heard.

The more I listened, the more I wanted to push back time. I wanted to go back to the first day of Honors Choir and start talking to Kathryn because she was sitting alone in the back row, not because Chloe had decided to have a stupid rush party. If I had met Kathryn on my own I could have stopped her from turning into this weird, fake person I barely knew. I could have told Chloe and the others that she was just another music freak. Pretended not to like her until I found a way of becoming a music freak myself—somebody none of them would ever give a crap about. I wanted to get Kathryn away from Chloe and everyone else who had nothing to do with music. And while I was getting Kathryn away, I wanted to get away, too.

"So what's on for tonight?" Chloe asked me. She dangled her flip-flops off her pedicured toes. "We doing a party or something else? Dina could come over. Maybe Angela, too."

I put a lie together quick. "Bill and Brice trashed the house last week. So Mom said no sleepovers for a month. Besides, I'm going to bed early."

"Why?" Chloe made a face. As if getting a good night's sleep was one of the stupidest things a person could do.

I waited to see if Kathryn would say something. She didn't, so I said it for her.

"Kathryn and I are going to the Blackmore tomorrow. Over at Baldwin. It starts at nine and goes all day. The finals aren't until eight or something."

Kathryn looked caught in the middle, but it was true. The two of us had been talking about the Blackmore since practically the day we'd met.

"I did tell Brooke I'd go with her, Chloe," she said.

Chloe gave the ice in her glass a ticked-off rattle. "So basically, what you're telling me is that you're leaving me stranded so you can go watch a bunch of people screech and scream all day. Thanks a lot."

The guilt trip almost worked, until I thought about how Kathryn and I hadn't done anything by ourselves in weeks. I scooted my chair around, so she and I were sitting closer together. "You could come," I told Chloe. "But I know how much you hate music freaks. So Kath and I'll just have to catch you later. Right, Kath?"

Kathryn went red again. She stared into her lemonade.

"Right."

Lake Champion changes completely when the festival comes around. Big banners go up all over campus. The light posts up and down Main Street get red, yellow, and orange streamers, and you start to see a lot of sophisticated people walking around—women with bobbed hair and men with pale skin, almost all of them dressed in black. There are reporters, talent scouts, and people who are such huge music fans that they don't mind traveling to the middle of nowhere if it means getting to hear the next Renée Fleming. Usually the celebrity judges stay to themselves, but sometimes you can catch one of them in the restroom. It's weird to see somebody you've watched

play a Valkyrie on TV washing their hands at the sink like everybody else.

And then you have the contestants. They come from all over the country—about a hundred of them in any given year. Up in the practice rooms, it's like a soup of different accents and even different languages, with everybody sizing everybody else up.

That morning Kathryn and I snuck in while the singers were still getting registered. We snagged two seats, right in the middle of the hall. For the first two rounds, singers are split between the main theater, the opera workshop theater, and one of the big choir rooms. Kathryn and I staked out the main venue. We ate granola bars and read the morning paper until it was time for the competition to start.

"Gee, I wonder who they're picking to win," I said, showing Kathryn the arts section. They'd done a huge spread on the competition with a map showing where everybody came from and profiles on the Douglas people who were competing that year. There were three from our school—Hannan Ameri, an alto; Beatrix Stahl, soprano; and Joel Graham, a tenor. They each got a write-up, but one of the articles was bigger than the rest. It took up half the page.

"Hannan," said Kathryn, reading over my shoulder. "I heard somebody came from Eastman just to hear her."

"I wonder if she's nervous," I said as the houselights went down. "I would be if it was me in that dress."

Hannan was first up, since rounds one and two are always alphabetical. There she was, the best singer at our school, wearing a purple evening gown with puffy sleeves at nine on a Saturday morning. It looked funny, but then everybody overdresses at the Blackmore. Because if you make it to the finals, then you don't look funny at all.

We sat superstill while Hannan sang her first two pieces. Halfway through the first one it was obvious something was wrong. She seemed tired. Jittery. Nothing about her performance was bad; something was just . . . missing. Kathryn fished a piece of paper and a pen out of her purse while Hannan took her bow. *Uh-oh,* she wrote.

An hour and a half later, Beatrix came on wearing a pink gown that showed off her end-of-summer tan. I pulled the crossword out of the paper and pretended to work it while she got ready to sing. Boring Beatrix. Kathryn swatted my hand. I yawned, not even bothering to cover my mouth. Kathryn giggled, and Beatrix nodded to let her accompanist know she was ready.

Her first piece was a Schubert lied. Nice, lyrical, and Beatrix made it look easy. Kathryn glanced at me out of the corner of her eye. Boring or not, Beatrix sounded better than most of the people we'd heard so far.

Then, she did something that made everybody gasp.

"No way!" Kathryn whispered as the pianist started the first, trilling notes to Bernstein's "Glitter and Be Gay."

"Glitter and Be Gay" is a total soprano showpiece. It's packed with vocal acrobatics. Not only that, but you have to act because it's a song about a hooker who feels bad about her life until she thinks about all the jewelry she's got, and then she gets insanely happy. Most high school singers wouldn't touch that song. If they did, it would be a finals piece because it's so showy. But Beatrix pulled it out for the first round.

"This could be bad," I whispered back. Except it wasn't. It was incredible. As Beatrix tore through the last, superhigh notes, you could feel the excitement building in the room. She was so on—so wild and polished all at the same time that I actually lost my breath for a minute. Shy, sappy Beatrix. Who knew she had it in her?

People started clapping before the pianist finished the last cadenza. By the time Beatrix took her bow, the applause was so loud that it felt like a thunderstorm.

"Wow," Kathryn shouted. All I could do was nod. Something special had just happened. I was glad I had her there to see it with me.

The whole morning went like that. Great singers.

Surprising performances. Kathryn and I passed snotty notes about the weak ones. We agreed instantly on who kicked ass. During breaks we talked about what we would do differently when *we* were the ones up on that stage. This was what I'd been missing—just me and Kathryn and music.

Just like it used to be.

Then, around three, she started checking her watch. She checked it while Hannan and Beatrix sang their second-round pieces. And she checked it while we walked to the coffee shop for dinner before the finals.

"How long do you think this will go?" she said as she hurried to keep up with me. We didn't have much time, and I wanted to make sure we could get our seats again when we got back to the hall.

It started to drizzle. I walked faster. "A couple of hours," I told her. "Depends how long the songs are." When we got inside it was crowded with people from the Blackmore—ushers, audience members, singers who'd already been eliminated. I couldn't imagine being able to eat after getting cut like that, but I saw at least five of them scattered around with their families. Some were even laughing.

We found two free seats at the end of a long table and Kathryn started flipping through her program, trying to see if it told what each finalist planned to sing. When she didn't find anything she looked up.

"Can I borrow your cell phone?"

"Why?" I said.

"I need to call Chloe."

That name made my blood stop. "Why do you need to call her?"

"She asked me to go out after the contest. I want to let her know I might be late."

There it was. The black again, turning what had been a great day into a sloppy, dark mess. I'd been hoping Kathryn and I could go back to my place after the Blackmore and listen to some CDs my dad had sent. I thought we'd talked about it earlier. But we either hadn't or it didn't interest her as much as going out with Chloe.

Kathryn didn't wait for me to hand her the phone. She just scooped it up and started texting.

"You're coming out, too, right?"

"No." I opened my menu. I wanted to get out of there fast, because I felt like I might actually cry.

"Why not?" said Kathryn. "It'll be fun. Chloe . . ."

I couldn't stand it anymore. "I'd watch out for Chloe if I were you," I snapped.

Her smile froze on her face. She flipped the phone shut.

"What? Why?"

"She's . . . just not all that nice all of the time." How

could I explain what I wanted to say without sounding like a petty, horrible friend? Chloe and I had been BFFs for almost six years. But when I looked back on it, I couldn't say exactly why. All of the plotting, the parties, the getting trashed, the A-list obsessions—Kathryn was better than that. And I wanted to be better than that, too.

But Kathryn just laughed.

"Chloe's been great to me, and she's your friend, so I'm sure she's fine. Right, Brooke?"

I fiddled with my napkin so I wouldn't have to look at her. I wanted Kathryn to believe me. More than that, I wanted her to want to be with me more than she wanted to be with Chloe. I was the one she had something in common with. I was her real friend. I wanted to lay it all out for her. Instead I just said, "Fine. Don't say I never warned you."

"Okay." She gave me a weird look. Then she picked up the phone and started texting again.

After that, things were awkward. We didn't talk much while we ate, or while we walked back for the finals. Onstage, things were even weirder. Hannan sounded more off than she'd been all day. Beatrix sounded even better, which was hard to believe if you knew her at all before the competition.

Obviously none of us had.

Kathryn and I watched while she accepted her first-place scholarship check and a huge bouquet of red lilies. We saw Hannan standing off to the side, trying to be gracious. But she looked pale and dazed. And when she moved forward to give Beatrix a hug, she almost dropped her fourth-place flowers. Kathryn nudged me to see if I'd noticed it and right then and there, I knew.

We were looking into the future.

Up until that minute, I had never really thought about what the Blackmore would mean for Kathryn and me. Now I realized that if one of us won, the other one would have to lose.

Maybe it was unavoidable that things would end up the way they did. Maybe we were going to end up as rivals no matter what happened to us junior year.

Maybe it just wouldn't have hurt so bad.

SENIOR YEAR

*Ostinato: stubborn—a musical phrase that repeats over
and over*

KATHRYN

"MATT, YOU ONLY HAVE A half hour before first bell."

Matt puts his cell phone down and goes back to his laptop, but not before checking the phone screen again.

"What?" he says when he catches me glaring. "The anime fen are tweeting from Dream Con. James Cameron just announced he's going to do a 3-D animated remake of *Gone with the Wind*!"

"But your column's due at the end of the day. If you don't turn it in, I end up with a huge hole in the features section."

Ben Sherman, the sports editor, glances over and gives me a sympathetic smile. A hole in your section is serious, especially when we don't have time for redos. It's seven thirty a.m. and the *Picayune* office is packed with staff squeezing in any time they can get to work on our regular paper plus the Homecoming edition, because even though Homecoming is weeks away, that paper is a keepsake and it takes a huge amount of resources to put out.

"Okay, okay," Matt says, shutting off his phone. "You're lucky you're such a cute slave driver."

I sigh and go back to helping Elise Cordry edit her feature on a Douglas girl who was selected to study at the School of American Ballet.

"I like how you describe her ballet classes," I tell her. "But I think you buried the lede a bit. See?" I point at the computer screen. "If you switch these two paragraphs it'll be more clear what the story's about."

Elise leans in and nods. "Yeah!" she says. "You're right!"

Out of the corner of my eye, I see a familiar figure come into the room. A few weeks ago, this particular person would barely have pinged my radar, but he's become a fixture of my mornings—my partner in fetal porcine mutilation.

John Moorehouse.

John high-fives Ben, then sits down next to Ben's computer station. He says hi to Matt, then I feel his gaze fall on me.

"Hey, Kathryn," he says. "What are you doing here?"

In spite of myself, I blush. It feels strange having him speak to me outside of Anatomy class. "I work here," I tell him.

"Kathryn's the features editor," Ben says.

"Dang." John regards me appreciatively. "Music, AP, the newspaper, what don't you do?"

"Um . . ." My tongue feels thick and clumsy. "Figure skating?" He laughs and so do Ben and Elise, and I start to feel more comfortable. "I should ask you the same thing," I say. "Why are you here when everybody else is chugging Starbucks in the commons?"

"Getting interviewed," John replies. "Sherman here insists on calling me the star quarterback, so apparently that makes everything I have to say really gripping. After that, I'm supposed to talk to your news editor for a story on King and Queen candidates."

I glance over at Matt, who's watching us over his laptop screen, a suspicious look on his face. I pretend to suddenly be interested in a hangnail, trying to make the whole thing seem like the not-big-deal that it really is. I mean, sure, the A-listers usually blatantly ignore me, but it isn't *that* odd to have one of them engage me in conversation.

Is it?

I suppose to Matt it is, considering that I never told him about John and me being lab partners. I don't know why, exactly—it's just that ever since John asked if Matt was my boyfriend, I've been a little more sensitive to what Matt might think; because if Matt is thinking about things like that, then it means that I have to think about them, too.

The office door opens and someone new walks in. Immediately, the energy in the room changes. I snap my attention back to my own computer.

"Dempsey!" John calls out. "You here for your Queen interview?"

"Yep," Brooke tells him. "I'm supposed to meet somebody in news. Are they here?"

Her gaze sweeps the room and, for a second, falls on me. I stare at my screen, pretending to be thoroughly engrossed in Elise's story, until—thank God—Erin LeGault, our news editor, stands up.

"Over here, Brooke!" she calls. "Thanks so much for coming in so early!"

Brooke goes over and sits down, and Erin launches into a set of questions. She asks Brooke about her chosen charity and Brooke's voice goes all soft and serious, as if she truly is concerned about rampant inequality within the music department.

"I've always thought it was unfair that singers are expected to pay for their gowns," she says. "I mean, the dresses cost a hundred and thirty dollars. To *most* people that's not a lot of money, but *some* people have a hard time just affording clothes for school, let alone a dress for music class."

I reach down and grab my backpack; I don't need to sit here and listen to this. The *Picayune* is one place where I actually sort of have friends—a safe, Brooke-free zone. If she's going to invade it, then I don't have to give her the satisfaction of sticking around.

"Go ahead and give the story one more pass, then turn it in for copyedits," I tell Elise. "You're in good shape."

I stand and hurry over to Matt.

"Come on," I whisper. "Let's go."

"But I'm not done with my column yet," he says. His cursor hovers over the "log off" icon as if waiting for permission to shut down. "What about your section hole?"

"I'll fill it with something else," I tell him. "Consider this an extension. Just please—let's get out of here."

BROOKE

THURSDAY NIGHT, I FINALLY GET an email
from Dad.

Honey, I'm so sorry I haven't gotten back to
you. San Francisco is insane, though the production looks amazing. I'm done next week and then
I'm moving on to—get this—Tulsa, Oklahoma. One
of their old patrons died and left a load of money
to the civic opera. They're doing *Madame Butterfly*,
only they're setting it in sixties Vietnam and it's just
too awful for words. I mean, why not just do *Miss
Saigon*? Anyway, I can't imagine you'd get much of
what you're looking for in Tulsa. If you want to go
to New York you can always stay in the apartment.
I can get recommendations for good coaches if you
need a foot in the door. Just let me know. Most of
my free time is during the day and I don't want to

interrupt your school, but I will try to call as soon as I can. I love you, Little Star!

I try not to be worried. Dad's really busy, and we've got plenty of time before the Blackmore. He always comes through, even if it's last-minute. Like the time when I was in eighth grade, playing the Artful Dodger in *Oliver!* It was my first real lead role. I was so excited I must have called Dad about it a hundred times. But by opening night I still hadn't heard from him. I waited right up until it was time to go on. Then I made myself accept that he probably wasn't coming. During intermission, though, I got a message from the stage manager that somebody was waiting for me in the greenroom. It was Dad and Jake. They'd come in during the overture and sat in the back so nobody would recognize them. I ran to Dad and let him pick me up.

"That was fantastic!" he said, and twirled me around. The stubble from his beard left marks in my greasepaint makeup. "I couldn't take my eyes off you!"

"Really?" I pulled off the old top hat I'd been wearing. "I almost forgot the words to 'Be Back Soon.'"

"Did you now? I couldn't tell." He put a kiss on my forehead. "My Little Star."

"Little?" said Jake with his big movie star voice. He was wearing sunglasses, even in the greenroom where nobody could see us. Which I guess just shows how nervous he was about getting recognized. "Why, she's big enough to play college basketball, aren't you, Brookie? How tall are you now? Six five? Six seven?"

Dad ignored Jake and gave me another twirl. "She's beautiful," he said. "Just beautiful."

When I turned back around, he had something in his hand. It was a little blue bag from Tiffany. I recognized it right away because he used to bring bags like that to my mom on special occasions. It was the first time he'd ever brought one for me.

I reached in and pulled out a tiny blue box. Inside was a silver star on a delicate chain.

"That's so you'll always have a little piece of me with you," he said. "So you'll always know I'm here, even if it doesn't seem like it."

I tried not to cry as he reached around and fastened the star behind my neck. Now, as I get in bed with the phone on the pillow next to me, I hold the star in my hand and tell myself everything is going to be okay.

But it doesn't make the next day any easier. I can't concentrate at school. I keep checking my cell for missed calls and text messages. By lunchtime I'm so antsy that I have to go home to check Mom's answering machine. Nothing. He probably stayed late at rehearsals. San Francisco is two hours behind us. He's probably still in bed.

We have nothing in the house for lunch but olives and frozen pizza, so I skip eating and head back to school. To choir, where—great timing!—I get to hear Kathryn sing her solo again. And now I'm closer to a meltdown than I ever was before. Because Kathryn is even better than she was the last time. The only hiccup is one high note that doesn't quite make it.

After class, Laura Lindner rushes down from the second sopranos.

"What a mess," she says while we're putting away our folders. "Kathryn, I mean. Is Anderson *trying* to screw us over?"

I walk to the door. Try to ignore her because what the hell does she know anyway? Out in the hallway, we run into Chloe.

"Hey, Chloe!" Laura says. "What's up?"

"I don't know," says Chloe. She looks pissed. "Why don't we ask Brooke?"

"Nothing's up," I tell them as we start down the hall. "At least I don't think there is."

"Now see, that's funny," Chloe says. "Because everybody else seems to know what's up. Laura, what is happening here in exactly three weeks and three days?"

"Homecoming," Laura answers.

"Right. And since you actually seem to be interested, maybe I can get you to help me out? Here." Chloe hands

162

Laura a chunk of papers from the stack in her hand. They are light blue and say BROOKE DEMPSEY FOR HOME-COMING QUEEN in big black letters.

"Crap," I say under my breath.

I totally forgot. Chloe and I were supposed to pass out campaign flyers today at lunch. Instead of meeting her I was at home, staring at a big, glowing *0 messages*.

"Chloe," I say, catching up as she sprints ahead. "Chlo. I'm sorry. My dad's helping me with the Blackmore, and I was trying to get hold of him at lunch. I just totally forgot."

She stops and hands some flyers, along with a hand-ful of bubble gum, to some Goth girls who are standing around an open locker. "Nothing to be sorry about. We'll just do it after school."

Ugh.

"I can't after school. I've got a voice lesson."

She's wearing her *you're not telling me this* face. She takes another handful of gum and shoves it at a fresh-man who's dumb enough to stumble in front of her. "Vote for Brooke!" she tells him.

"Hey, Chloe . . ." I reach out for the bag of gum, trying to at least *look* like I might reconsider and do the after-school thing. She stops walking and yanks it away.

"No, Brooke!" Her voice is too sharp. A couple of people look over and she speaks more quietly. "Some

people would kill to be where you are right now, but you obviously don't give a crap about this. And I don't know if it's a good thing or just incredibly sad that you'd probably win even if they took your name off the ballot."

"Chloe . . ." I can tell she's hurt, and I want to be a good friend. Really. But there's no way I'm skipping my voice lesson. Not with all the work I still have to do for the Blackmore.

"I'm going to class," she says, tossing a piece of bubble gum at my chest. "And hey, since you're probably the only person on earth who has to be reminded, vote for Brooke!"

My voice lesson did not go well. Hildy asked me which pieces I wanted to perform for the Blackmore, and I told her I hadn't made a final decision yet. I told her about my dad working in San Francisco. How I wanted to get his opinion before I nailed anything down, and she went off on me. She told me I don't have any new "showpieces" in my repertoire. And without one of those I might as well kiss first place good-bye. She gave me five songs to look at. I told her I'd work on all of them and have two picked out by my lesson next week.

Now I'm home, trying to reach my mom, who's AWOL, too. For the past few weeks she's been working late every night. In meetings, where she can't even use her cell phone. I'm typing her an email when all of a sudden she shows up on IM.

MDEMPSEY: Interview w/10 p.m. news—did you need me?
BROOKLYN_11: I need to go to NYC
MDEMPSEY: When?
BROOKLYN_11: Soon—next wk
MDEMPSEY: Will your dad be there?

I want to type "yes." But I know I have to tell the truth because she'll find out either way.

BROOKLYN_11: No but I'll stay in the apt. I'm going to sing
MDEMPSEY: Not alone and I can't take you

I smack my hand on top of my desk. She acts like I've never been to New York before. Like I didn't practically grow up there. Did she not get it when I said I was going there to sing?

BROOKLYN_11: Blackmore = most imp contest of my life— why RU giving me shit?

Her next message contains nothing but a link. I click

on it. It's a story from the local paper. The name of her bank is there in the headline, next to the word "merger."

> MDEMPSEY: Other people have important things going on too
> BROOKLYN_11: I'm going
> MDEMPSEY: With what $?
> BROOKLYN_11: Dad & Jake will help
> MDEMPSEY: Don't count on it

Tears of frustration burn my eyes. I'm surprised, and dead set on keeping them back. My mom would love it if I never did anything else but go to parties and hang around Lake Champion. She missed out on the whole high school thing because she was building herself up as a singer, meeting guys like my dad who worked in Broadway theaters. She got to live that life, but she doesn't want me to—and it's totally, completely not fair.

> BROOKLYN_11: Ur ruining my life—i hate you

It takes her forever to reply. When she finally does, it's a whole paragraph typed out with perfect grammar. Which means she's really mad.

> MDEMPSEY: I am not going to defend myself to you after

I've worked so hard to keep some security in your life, and not while you're sitting at home enjoying the computer and the house that I pay for with virtually no help from your father considering how well off he is these days. If you want understanding, I suggest you try understanding a few things yourself. Good night.

I log off IM. Pull up the internet and start checking travel sites. There's a cheap flight to LaGuardia that leaves Saturday morning. I start to click on the reservation, then stop. I'd have to ask Dad for the money, and how can I guarantee I'd even get hold of him in time?

Downstairs, someone is knocking on the front door. I'm not in the mood to entertain somebody from school who just decided to drop by. But the knocking keeps up, so I sneak down and peek through the front-door window.

It's Chloe.

"Let me in," she says through the glass. "We've got work to do."

I undo the dead bolt, and she pushes by with a stack of magazines in her arms. She's halfway up the stairs before I've gotten the door closed. Up in my room, she flips on the overhead light. "We have to find you a Homecoming gown. Unless you'd rather shop off the rack."

She drops the magazines on my desk, flops onto her

stomach on my bed, and starts surfing on my laptop while I stand in the doorway. I could tell her to go home. That I want to be alone. But I feel bad about earlier.

"I thought you were mad at me," I say.

"I am mad. But I know you, Brooke. If I didn't force you to pay attention to this stuff, you'd spend all your time on music and show up to Homecoming in a feed sack." She Googles the designer who just won *Project Runway*, then surfs over to the site and starts clicking through the dresses. "Now, if it was me, I'd wear . . ."

I sit next to her. Look over her shoulder and watch the totally focused and determined way she sorts through all the possibilities. Say what you like about Chloe, but she's scary good at getting what she wants, even if she has to get it some roundabout way that nobody expects. Like in sixth grade. I don't remember actually meeting or choosing her. She was just always there—like she'd chosen *me* and had made up her mind that we were going to be best friends.

What I do remember is the way she talked about her family. She told anybody who would listen that her mom had married a rich guy. That he was a big deal at his job and was probably going to be famous someday. She loved talking about all the stuff he bought for her and bragging about the cool places they went on vacations. I never thought to question it because Chloe made the stories so believable.

One day Mom made me go with her on one of her PR projects. The bank wanted to do a profile on someone they'd helped, and Mom was supposed to interview single parents at Baldwin who were getting by with loans. She dragged me through the student apartments, in and out of these tiny places where young couples and their kids were living on practically nothing while the parents went to class and worked extra jobs to make ends meet. By the time we got to the last one, I was so tired and depressed I wanted to keel over. The lady who answered the door looked like she hadn't slept in a week, and the only things I could see inside her apartment were a futon, a television, and a laptop with a stack of books on the kitchenette island.

"Let me get my daughter," the woman said to me. "She's just about your age."

She went down a little hallway and knocked on a door. It opened, and a girl poked her head out. The girl looked at my mom and me. Her eyes got big. She shook her head at the woman and shut the door again while I stood there, quietly freaking out.

It was Chloe.

"I don't know what's gotten into her," the woman said as she came back to the living room. "She probably isn't feeling well."

Chloe never talked about that day, and I was too weirded out to bring it up. She also never changed her story. Because eventually? It all came true. Her mom did marry a rich guy, and he did get famous—at least as far as politics go. By eighth grade, Chloe really was jetting off to incredible vacation spots, and she had a clothes allowance that made even me jealous. It was almost like she'd made it all happen, just by wanting it.

And now, she's trying to make it happen for me, even though I know she's imagining herself in the sash and tiara.

"Why *aren't* you on the court?" I ask her. "You're the one who really cares about Homecoming."

"Because I'm just not, okay?" She flips another page and, for a second, I see that big-eyed little girl again. "I'm happier behind the scenes, Brooke," she tells me. "But I can't do anything if you don't help out a little. You're never around anymore. What's the deal?"

"The Blackmore," I remind her. "It's next month."

She rolls onto her back and looks at me, very serious. "Why is this contest thing so important anyway? You've always been weird about singing, but you're really freaking out this year."

"I'm not freaking out."

"Oh my God, you are *so* freaking out. Why? You're going to get the big first-place star part or whatever it is

you want. You always do."

I lie down, grab one of her magazines, and start flipping. But it's just something to do with my hands while I come out and say what's really bothering me. "Maybe not always," I say.

Chloe snorts. "What? Who else is going to get it?"

"This contest has some of the best singers in the country," I explain. "You can't assume anything at the Blackmore. The competition is really fierce."

She waves her hand like she's swatting pesky flies, and any hope I might have had of her understanding starts to fade. I guess I've known all along that she's not the person to talk to about stuff like this. But I can't just drop the subject. I need to talk with somebody. "And then," I say, "there's Kathryn."

"Don't worry about Kathryn."

She says it like it's simple. Like I can just snap my fingers and make Kathryn disappear.

"It's not that easy," I tell her.

Chloe wrinkles her nose. "Why not?"

"Well, for one thing, I see her every day in choir."

"So? Ignore her."

"I try to. But . . ."

"But what?" Chloe's eyes are mean little slits now. "You're you and she's nobody."

"She's getting solos and I'm not."

"So let her have them. Is she up for Homecoming Queen? Is she even going to Homecoming?"

"I don't think she cares about stuff like that."

"Of course she cares. Believe me, Brooke. Homecoming is way more interesting than some singing contest."

That finally shuts me up. Because Chloe doesn't get it, and she never will. It's best to just let her deal with the things she does get, so I flip another page and point at the first dress I see.

"Too old lady-ish," she says. "How about this one?" She points to a pink, floor-length gown with sparkles all over it.

"What am I, Glinda the Good Witch? It's going to be, like, ten below out. And we'll be on a muddy football field."

"Oh yeah," she says. "Right. What about vintage?"

I perk up, picturing movie stars on a red carpet. "But vintage always runs small. I'll never find something that fits."

I flip some more and finally find a black sheath dress that has a little bow just underneath the breastline. It comes with a deep red cashmere shrug, so it's got long sleeves if you need them. Best of all, it won't look too bad if it gets wet or muddy. "What about this?" I say.

Chloe moves my finger away from the picture so she can see it better. "John Moorehouse will love it."

172

My heart *ka-thumps* in my chest. I shove her almost all the way off the bed.

"Shut up!"

"Why?" She giggles. "It's obvious you like him."

"Obvious to who?" Now I've got visions of the whole school talking about me and my huge, stupid crush. And what if *John* knows? I will die. Unless he's happy because he likes me, too. In which case I will really die. But in a good way.

"I'm the only one who's noticed," Chloe says. "And that's just because nothing gets past the amazing, all-seeing Chloe. Now relax!"

I can't, though. Because John Moorehouse is pretty much the only thing I've been able to think about lately. Well, besides the Blackmore. And Kathryn. And my dad.

"Keep it to yourself," I warn her.

"That won't be easy when the whole school sees you together at Homecoming."

And now we're there, where I secretly wanted to go but have been too afraid to admit. I can't talk to Chloe about music, but I can talk to her about this. So I say what's been on my mind for days now.

"He hasn't asked me."

"He will."

"How do you know?"

"Trust me," she says. "He's busy with football right

now. He'll ask you."

I put my chin in my hand, trying to imagine what that will be like. Will he call? Or will he grab me in the hallway at school? Will he come right out and ask? Or will he do something romantic, like bring roses?

"Whatever he's planning, he'd better do it soon," I say.

"Don't worry." Chloe finds the black dress online and pulls up a form for a shop in Minneapolis that carries it. "You guys are the two most popular people in school. It's perfect. Exactly the way I would have done it."

KATHRYN

"ANYBODY CAN WRITE."

Ms. Amos, my AP English teacher, is stalking back and forth in front of the classroom, her stiletto heels clicking on the old tile floor. Our last few papers have not been up to par, and she is laying out her expectations while my classmates and I scribble furiously in our notebooks.

"English is about more than just words," she tells us. "It's about finding new ways to illuminate and make sense of the mysteries and minutiae of daily existence. Yes, I want you to write flawlessly, but I also want you to be original; otherwise, why bother?"

I write down the word "flawless" and underline it twice; I write the word "original" and highlight it with a star. Then I look down into my backpack, at the folder where I keep the music for my voice lessons; tucked inside it are six new pieces that Mr. Lieb gave me yesterday.

"Learn them all, and we'll see which ones fit best," he'd said. "You're in good shape for the first two rounds, especially with the coloratura we've been working on, but you'll need a showstopper for the finals. I've always been partial to this one." He pointed to the aria on top of the stack, titled "The Jewel Song" from the opera *Faust*. It's an acting piece—about a peasant girl who receives an enchanted box of diamonds and laughs at her reflection as she tries them on before a mirror.

Plus, the song is in French.

"It's . . ." My throat suddenly felt very dry. "It's really advanced."

"Well, you aren't going to win this with 'Caro Mio Ben.'"

"I know," I murmured. Though I could tell he didn't mean to hurt me, the remark still stung; I could only imagine the vocal fireworks Brooke has planned. Mr. Lieb reached up from the piano and put his hand on my music, coaxing it down so his eyes could meet mine.

"If I didn't think you could do this I wouldn't have given it to you," he said. "You're going to be wonderful. I have nothing but faith in you."

Faith, I think now as I stare at the music in my backpack. *I'm going to need a lot of that.*

Especially if I don't find some time to practice. Between AP English, the *Picayune,* Human Anatomy, and all of my other classes, I've been staying up late, spending afternoons at the library and carving out a half hour here, forty-five minutes there for singing. That's no way to prepare for a competition like the Blackmore, but I can't seem to figure out a way to get everything done. Today, for example, I should go home and spend a good couple of hours on the new pieces Mr. Lieb gave me; instead, I head to the library to do some research for Ms. Amos and use their internet connection, which is a lot faster than the one we have at home.

On my way in I bump into Laura Lindner, who stands alone by the magazine racks. I venture a "hello," only to be answered with a glare as Laura turns and stalks off to the back corner, where a group has laid claim to the tables. The schedule at the checkout desk says the Spirit Committee is meeting today, and sure enough, there is Chloe Romelli talking to Tyrone Marshall, the new Douglas mascot. Chloe's voice, which has always been loud, gets louder as she talks about which florist she's planning to hire for bouquets. "I want everyone to look beautiful," she says. "I don't care if Homecoming is some philanthropy thing now, I'm not going to stick my friends with tacky blue carnations."

I duck into a computer station, log in to the online card catalog, and type in "Theater of the Absurd." A little clock appears on the screen, its hands spinning while the computer processes my request. The hands spin and spin; I try to get another window so I can start the search again, but nothing happens. I slide over to the next station and try again. More spinning. I glance around at the other computers and realize that I'm the only one trying to use them; they must all be down, which means I am either going to have to search the old-fashioned way or ask for help.

Leaving my things at my seat, I hurry over to the librarian's desk. Her computer has crashed, too, so I wait while she flips through the yellowed card catalog, and then make my way to the shelves where the books I want are located. I return to my computer with three, open my bag to put them in, and there, tucked between my music and my English notes, is a slip of paper that wasn't there before.

I pull it out and unfold it; it's a print of the famous painting of a drowned Ophelia with my face Photoshopped where hers should be. In the picture, my eyes stare creepily at the sky, hair billowing in the water, palms turned upward. I look around and immediately my eye goes to the Spirit Committee. They're deep into their meeting now, with Chloe recording minutes in an official-looking notebook.

The picture wasn't in my bag before, I'm sure of that, and I don't see anybody else in the library who could have put it there. In case somebody is watching, I pretend like nothing's happened and I'm just going about my usual business.

Inside, though, I am buzzing with shock as I gather my things and hurry out to the parking lot. Nearing my car, I see something hanging off of the rear antenna—an inflated inner tube, the kind that kids use. It is bright blue with little red fish swimming across the top, and somehow the brightness makes it even more sinister, especially when I read the note taped to it: *You never know when you might need this.*

I snatch the tube off and fling it into my backseat. Then, on the way home, I stop behind a Burger King and leave it in one of the Dumpsters. The nerve behind my right eye has begun to throb; if I don't take aspirin soon, the headache will take hold and last for days.

I arrive home to the smell of fried chicken and venture into the kitchen to find the table set with mashed potatoes, Brussels sprouts, and crusty butter rolls. Dad already sits in his place, thumbing through a packet of papers that I recognize as a statement from the guy who manages his retirement fund. He sighs, folds up the papers, and tosses them onto the counter as I sit across from him. Mom starts spooning food onto my plate, so quiet that I know something is going on; I discover what it is when I reach for my napkin and find three envelopes tucked underneath.

"I have a good feeling about these," Mom tells me. "I was going to open them, but I thought you would want to do it yourself."

I sit for a moment, looking at the envelopes. My hand hovers over the top one, which bears the seal of a school where I applied for a journalism scholarship.

"You don't have to open it now. Go ahead and eat first," says Mom. But I know she and Dad have probably been counting the minutes until they can see what's inside, so I cool my throat with a sip of milk and start to open.

I open the first, then the second, then the third, looking over the contents quickly as if skimming will make it any less painful. It's more of the same: minuscule scholarships and invitations to sing for the voice faculty again once I've completed my first year. One school rejects me altogether; apparently neither my writing nor my singing meets their standards.

"I just don't understand it," says Mom. "Your grades are excellent. You sang for the president, for goodness' sake. Who in the world is getting these scholarships if it isn't you?"

I sit miserably, picking the skin off my chicken, eating the crispies because I can't resist them but feeling nauseous at the meat underneath; after four weeks of dissecting a fetal pig, I can identify nearly every muscle on the drumstick.

"Kathryn doesn't need a scholarship," Dad says. "There are other forms of financial aid."

"Loans you mean." Mom's knuckles are white as she grips the serving spoon, plopping mashed potatoes onto her plate in big, angry dollops. "I'm not letting our daughter start out with the kind of debt we had. We said we'd do better than that."

"Mom . . ." I hate it when they talk like this. "Something will come through." Smiling weakly, they go back to their food and a vague notion I've had for the past few weeks comes suddenly into focus: Neither of them has mentioned the Blackmore to me. At first, when I didn't want them to know I'd entered, their silence was a relief; but all this time has gone by, and they still haven't said anything. Surely they know by now that it's still on. It's only the biggest thing to happen to this town every year, and now it's an even bigger deal because of all the drama surrounding the new recital hall. If they know it's coming up, then they have to know it's something I'd participate in. There has to be a reason they aren't talking about it with me.

Maybe they don't think I can win. Maybe they're trying to save me even more disappointment.

The possibility of this is worse than the great expectations I'd originally feared; it's like they've given up before I've even had the chance to try.

"May I be excused?"

Mom looks at my plate, worried.

"You've barely eaten anything. Don't you want dessert?"

"No," I tell her. "I have a headache." I take a bottle of aspirin from the cupboard above the sink, shake out three, and wash them down with the rest of my milk. "I'm going up to do homework."

On my way through the living room I pass our old piano, which crouches in the corner like it expects something from me. I desperately need to practice but the piano is out in the open where everybody can hear, and the atmosphere is so tense that there's no way I'll be able to concentrate.

I go upstairs, take the cordless into my bedroom, and dial.

"Hold everything," Matt says when he hears my voice. "I'll be right over."

"Guacamole. Good for whatever ails you."

Matt smiles with satisfaction as a waitress puts a bowl of green dip on the table between us. He's brought me to our favorite Mexican restaurant, the one with the tinted windows that tempt passersby to stop and admire themselves, not realizing until it's too late that they're putting on a show for a dining room filled with people. We started coming here when we were finally old enough to go places by ourselves, and over time it became *our* place.

Matt scoops some guacamole with a tortilla chip and tries to hand it to me. I wave it away, pointing instead to the picture of Ophelia on the table between us.

"It's like she's stalking me. Like she actually wants me dead."

Matt studies the picture. "You didn't see her in the library? Are you sure she wasn't there?"

"She didn't need to be there. Brooke Dempsey has people who wait in line to do her bidding."

Matt scrunches up his forehead, then he flips the paper over, blank side up, and pushes it back across the table. "You're right," he says. "It sucks. But who wants to talk about sucky things when you've got avocados, sour cream, and a little bit of jalapeño pepper, hmmm?" His frown morphs into a smile as he dips another chip and waves it in front of my face. The smell from the onions almost makes me gag.

"I can't," I tell him. "Not hungry."

"You have to eat something. You'll make yourself sick."

"I already am sick. I've got a headache and way too much to think about."

"Then think about something trivial."

"Something like . . . ?"

"Like . . ." He whistles as he thinks. "Like Homecoming! What?" he says when I roll my eyes. "I thought girls loved that kind of thing."

"Some girls."

"You're not a 'some girl'?"

"I'm a 'no girl' as far as Homecoming is concerned." Just to make him happy, I grab a chip and nibble at the corners. "You and I will go together because neither of us has anything better going on. We'll get a pizza, head over to the game for the last quarter, and then hang out at the dance until we're bored. Then we'll go back to my house and fall asleep in front of the TV."

He takes the half-eaten chip out of my hand, dips it, and hands it back. "So what's wrong with that?"

"Absolutely nothing. It is what it is." I stick my tongue into the creamy guacamole, letting the flavor spread across my tongue; the guacamole *is* good, and now that I've tried it I realize that I really am hungry. I gobble the dip and the chip together, then reach for another.

"What if I did something special this year?" Matt says. "Buy you flowers, say. Or maybe wear a suit?"

A piece of chip goes down the wrong way, setting off a hacking fit.

Is Matt your boyfriend?

No. I can't go there, at least not tonight; tonight I

need him to just be my friend. I grab my water and take a sip.

"Don't you dare!" I croak. "The last thing I need is a reminder of the complete and utter lack of romance in my life."

"Okay, okay," he says. "It was just a thought."

"Well, save your thoughts for my AP English paper. I have to come up with something flawless and original. And I haven't even started on the ridiculously hard piece Mr. Lieb gave me for the Blackmore. Then there's State choir regionals . . ."

"You know, Kath, it's okay to let a few things slide every once in a while. You don't have to do it all."

Once again, my appetite vanishes. For someone who knows me so well, sometimes I am amazed at how much Matt doesn't understand.

"What am I supposed to let slide?" I ask. "My grades, which I need to get money for college? Regionals, where the entire Honors Choir is relying on me to not foul everything up? The Blackmore, which is starting to look like my last chance to keep my parents out of massive debt? And oh look! Now we're back to money for college again."

I put my head in my hands. My right eye throbs, and I press the tip of my tongue between my teeth so I'll have a different kind of pain to think about.

"What can I say, Kath?" Matt says. "It's high school. It won't last forever."

"Well, how about I check out until it's over? I could use an eight-month nap."

"I'd miss you," he says, taking the check from our waitress before I have the chance to grab it. "Besides, I've always liked having you to myself."

Today the headache is worse. All morning I'm a dizzy, nauseated mess, and to top it all off, when I get to choir I find a CPR manual for lifeguards in my folder. YOU CAN SAVE SOMEONE FROM DROWNING! it says. I'm dying to go home, but Ms. Burke has an Anatomy study session scheduled for after school, so I take three aspirin, sleep in my car through sixth period, and then go on to the lab.

"You okay?" The concern in John Moorehouse's voice tells me exactly how out of it I must seem.

"Honestly?" I say. "Not really."

"Hm . . ." He studies me, and I can see faint smudges of black under his eyes from the football practice he had to leave in order to make it here on time. "Your left eye looks like it's stuck in a permawince. Your pupils are dilated, and you're hunching like it hurts to move your neck. I diagnose a migraine."

"Is it that obvious?" I squeeze my eye shut and then

open it again—now that he's mentioned it I guess I really have been wincing all day.

"I get them, too," John says. "Does it feel like somebody's blowing up a balloon—right here?" He touches his fingers lightly, first to the spot where my eye meets the bridge of my nose, and then to my temple. It should probably make me uncomfortable, but his fingertips are cool, and the places where they've been are actually pain-free for a moment.

"That's exactly what it's like," I tell him.

"Yeah," he replies. "I don't think it's all in your head."

"Oh, I know I'm not imagining it."

"No, I mean you've got so much going on right now." He waves his scalpel over our pig, then in a bigger circle, at everything around us. "I know *I'm* maxing out on the recommended daily dosage of Excedrin before I even make it to football every day."

"That sucks," I say.

He shrugs. "I guess that's our reward for being overachievers." He turns back to our pig and points at a muscle in the leg. "Now what's this? The semitendinosus or the semimembranosus?"

"Ummm . . . I don't know. Let me see."

I go to the textbook and start flipping pages; when I look up, a piece of paper is tacked to the muscle in question with one of the pins that Ms. Burke uses to hold back skin so we can identify the organs underneath.

Want to go to Homecoming? it says.

"What's this?" I ask.

"What?" says John.

"This." I point to the piece of paper.

"Oh, that! Well, that's a question. Do you want to go?"

"With you?"

He looks around. "Um, yeah! Who else?"

I wait for his smile to turn into a sneer. John may be one of the few people I know who understands the agonies of a migraine, but he's also an A-lister.

His smile begins to falter.

"You're serious?" I say.

"I wouldn't have asked if I wasn't." He unpins the note and crumples it. "But it's cool if you don't want to. I just thought . . ."

"No, it's just . . ." I pause; last year was the first time I had a real Homecoming date, and I've mostly blocked that out, because who wants to remember one of the most humiliating nights of their life?

"Don't act too excited or anything," John says. He looks truly hurt now, and I remember just last night, complaining about how nobody wanted to go with me. Now, one of the best-looking guys at school is asking me out.

Why is he asking me out?

"No!" I say. "I mean, yes. I'm excited. Just ignore me. I'm not feeling well, remember?"

"Does that mean you'll go?"

"Yes," I say, because his uncertain eyes with those black smudges underneath them truly are adorable and because, after the water toys and the notes and the worry about Brooke on top of everything else, it feels good to be wanted.

"Great." He looks relieved. "We'll meet up after the game, go to the dance, maybe get something to eat after that. It'll be fun."

It does sound nice; and for the first time in what seems like weeks, I smile and really mean it.

"That's more like it," he says. He points at a long muscle inside the pig's thigh. "Now, what is this damned thing?"

"The semimembranosus," I say. It turns out I didn't have to look it up after all.

BROOKE

"ALL RIGHT NOW, NICE AND easy. Start here and slide up the octave, then back down, keeping the tone resonant in your nasal cavity. Let's do it softly, and . . ."

I'm standing in the crook of Hildy Shultz's piano, warming up at the start of my voice lesson. She gives me the beginning note, and I open my mouth to do the exercise. Nothing comes out. I put in a bit more breath and get a tone. But it's hoarse. Like I've got a cold.

"Stop," says Hildy after I've tried a few more times. "Brooke, are you feeling all right?"

I tell her I am. It's the truth. I don't feel sick, even though I sound like I'm trying to sing through a nasty sore throat. It's like my voice box is swollen. The sound is having trouble getting out.

"Try this," Hildy says. She leads me through some vocalises that go from what should be my lowest tone to what should be my highest. I can only get the middle register out. And even those notes sound forced.

"Okay, stop. Open." Hildy stands up, leaning over so she can examine the back of my mouth. She pulls back and glares at me. "I admire your dedication, Brooke, but you need to let up a bit. You're abusing your voice."

"I'm being careful," I tell her. "I don't scream or sing outside my range or anything like that."

"But how often are you singing? In addition to your regular practicing, are you having extra rehearsals in choir?" She can tell by the look on my face what my answers are. The look on her face tells me she doesn't like it. "I'm stopping this lesson right here," she says. "There's no point in going on if you don't have a voice, plus you need to take a break." She pulls a sheet of paper from a pad on her music stand and writes down a phone number. "This is for Dr. Dunne. He's the ear, nose, and throat specialist who sees all the students here. Get an appointment as soon as you can and *take it easy* for a few days. Let's hope you haven't given yourself polyps. Or nodes, God forbid."

Leaving her office feels like getting kicked out. Nodes are a singer's worst fear. They're bumps that form on your vocal cords when you abuse them, like blisters or calluses, and they keep the folds of muscle from vibrating together right. Nodes can ruin your career. A lot of times the only way to get rid of them is surgery. But that can damage your voice even more.

Now I'm really freaked out, and I have no idea what to do with myself. I don't want to go home. The place is too quiet with Mom working late all the time, and if I can't practice, then I don't really want to be there. But if I call Chloe, then we'll end up someplace like Pomodori's or a party, and I'll have to yell over the noise, which will only make my voice worse.

Bang, bang, bang . . . Out in the atrium, they've put up tape around the entrance to the new hall where the Blackmore is supposed to take place. Inside, construction workers are banging around under utility lamps. I step over the tape and peek around the corner. There's no way it'll be finished in time. The theater looks like I feel—ripped up and totally unprepared.

I walk across the atrium and up the stairs to the second floor, where the practice rooms are lined up in one long hallway. It sounds like an orchestra warming up—lots of people singing and playing instruments, everybody working on something different. The rooms are supposed to be soundproof, but you can hear a lot through the doors. Like the soprano three rooms down.

I walk up closer, trying to tune out the other noises. The voice is sweet but powerful. So clear and focused I can hear every word, even through the practice room door.

It's Kathryn. Has to be.

The piece she's working on is fast, with lots of high notes jumping around, and she's having trouble with it. She starts a passage, stops, then starts again. She skips to another spot in the song, but that part is hard, too. She tries it out a few times, and then there's silence. I go up to the door and put my ear close. Behind the thick wood I can hear a sniffle, then soft crying.

I should be happy she's upset. But what I really feel is a tired kind of sympathy. I step away from the door and leave her alone.

Back downstairs, on the other side of the music wing, I test the door to the theater where the opera workshop rehearses. It's unlocked. So I go inside and sit in the back row where nobody will see me. They're working on *The Turn of the Screw*, which is based on the book about a nanny and two possessed children. I shut my eyes and listen like I've done so many times before, trying to see if there's anything I can learn. But all I can think of is that the singers I'm hearing are stuck. Because if you really want to make a career out of this you don't come to Lake Champion, Minnesota. You come here if you want to teach or maybe direct choirs, but not if you're serious about singing. For that you go to a big city. Ian Buxton Blackmore must have realized that. Everybody talks about the Blackmore like he started it so people could come and hear all of the great singers in Lake Champion. I think he really created it so singers like me could get *out*.

The door on the other side of the theater opens and somebody comes in. The person sits down against the far wall. Even though it's dark I can tell from the outline of her ponytail that it's Kathryn. She looks tinier than ever, and just as lost as me.

Sitting across from each other in the dark, I start to wonder—would it be weird if I went and sat next to her? What would I say? What would she do?

I come close to getting up and going over. But every time, something holds me back. Kathryn and I have been enemies for a year now. How do you fix something like that? And do I even want to after all that happened?

Every time I look at her, it still feels like yesterday.

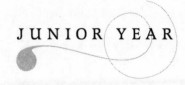

JUNIOR YEAR

Bellicoso: to be performed in an aggressive, warlike fashion

KATHRYN

MOST PEOPLE, IF THEY BECAME popular overnight, would probably revel in a newfound sense of importance. They'd enjoy the envious glances of those who weren't so lucky, the exclusive parties, the new view from the A-list bench in the commons. For me, the best thing about junior year was the freedom. I soon realized that nothing I did with Brooke or Chloe or Dina would ever go on my transcript. And when my mom and dad asked about all of the time we spent together, I found it surprisingly easy to lie—even when my grades started to slip.

"I'm sure this is an abnormality," said my Trigonometry teacher, Mr. Boyd, as he handed me yet another D+ test. *Discuss with your parents,* he'd scrawled along the bottom. *Perhaps you need a tutor.*

But I didn't discuss it with them; I hid the exam in my dresser drawer along with two barely passing English essays. I had better things to think about; things like the Senior Keg.

After weeks of suspense, Miles finally got me an invitation, along with permission to bring one other person. I chose Chloe because Brooke was already going with her brothers, who'd decided to come back just for the party. But Miles couldn't drive us because he had to be there early, so Bill and Brice offered to take everyone instead.

"We'll be the only nonseniors there," Chloe told me as we waited on the front steps of her house for them to show up. "Except for the college kids, of course. This is practically a college party!" Bouncing with excitement, she tucked a stray hair beneath the brim of the hat that coordinated perfectly with her powder blue ski jacket.

I shivered, pulling my old peacoat closer around my body. "Is it really going to be outside? What do people *do*? It's so cold!"

"Not if you have supplies." Chloe took a small thermos out of her bag. She unscrewed the cap, took a swig, and then handed it to me. Coffee-scented steam rose from inside, heavy with the rich smell of liquor. "Espresso and Bailey's Irish Crème," she said as I brought it to my lips. The hot coffee warmed my mouth and throat; the alcohol warmed the rest of me.

Lights appeared at the end of Chloe's driveway. She

put the thermos away as a Jeep drove up with Bill in the driver's seat, Brice sitting next to him and Brooke in the back.

"Tell Monaghan he owes me," Bill joked as we slid in. "The Dempsey cab service ain't cheap."

"Actually, I think he owes *me*," I teased back. "This isn't exactly a limo."

Bill laughed, and Brice and Chloe did, too. I thought I heard Brooke mutter something under her breath, but the CD player was up too loud.

We were quiet, and for a few songs it was okay; then a melancholy ballad started and my fear of long silences got the best of me.

"So this party is at The Rocks," I said. "Why do they call it that?"

"You've never been out to The Rocks?" Bill eyed me in the rearview mirror.

"Kathryn's a virgin," Chloe announced.

"So are you," said Brooke, making Chloe's know-it-all tone sound downright friendly.

"I've been to The Rocks before," Chloe said.

"In the afternoon. To lay out. That doesn't really count, does it?"

Chloe fell quiet, pouting, and Brooke glared straight ahead. This had been happening more and more often: She would be closed-lipped and snappish, and when anybody asked what was wrong, she would say "nothing."

While I prayed for another loud song to come on, Brice turned in his seat. "Brooke," he said. "Hand me a beer."

Brooke just sat there with her arms crossed. It was Chloe who finally reached into the cooler behind our seats and brought out bottles for Brice, herself, and me. As I took the first sip, I noticed Brooke glaring at me.

"Do you want one?" I said.

"No," she replied.

"Are you feeling okay?"

"I feel fine." She turned to the window, leaving me to stare at her shoulders. Outside, the road grew narrow, winding through trees that loomed up on either side like black spires. Bill rounded a curve, and the trees opened abruptly into a clearing. Parked cars stretched out before us, and beyond them we could see bodies illuminated by random headlights and the glow of a huge bonfire.

We left the Jeep at the edge of the lot and followed the twins to an old pickup where a keg had been set up on the flatbed.

"Awesome," said Chloe as Bill shelled out five dollars each for red plastic cups, which he distributed among us. Brooke took one, but while the rest of us held ours under the spigot, she spun around and started walking toward the bonfire. I saw her drop her cup as we hurried to join her.

"Don't you want any?" I said, ready to share. The air was frigid, and I didn't feel like drinking something cold on top of it.

"No," she snapped.

"Whatever," said Chloe as Brooke walked on ahead of us. "She'll be bare-assed by midnight."

"Really?" I watched as Brooke greeted some seniors around the bonfire; in her leather barn jacket and scarf she looked much older than a junior.

"You mean she hasn't told you about that time at Steak 'n' Shake? Or Dan Hummel and the Mardi Gras beads? Oh my God, Brooke is the queen of getting trashed and nasty."

Chloe gave me the whole story as we cleared the final feet to the fire's edge. I barely believed it—I'd never seen Brooke so much as take a sip of alcohol, let alone do something as undignified as throwing up or getting naked in public. I envied how good it must feel to be free enough to do things like that, even if they *were* embarrassing.

The seniors moved back as we approached, letting us through. "Hey, Kathryn," said Nick Zimmerman, and I nearly spilled my beer in surprise. The student council president actually knew my name! I finished my drink, then let Chloe refill my cup from her thermos. Minutes later somebody new came by, handing out shots of whiskey.

"Careful," Brooke said as I puckered at my first taste of Jack Daniel's. "You don't have much of a tolerance, I bet."

The warmth had spread from my stomach to my cheeks, and little sparks of I didn't know what were starting to flash inside of me—excitement and daring and new possibilities. I washed down the whiskey with a chug of spiked coffee.

"I'm okay," I told her. "You don't have to babysit."

I meant it to sound like a joke but I think she took it the wrong way, because she said "fine," and then disappeared into the dark. Stunned and disoriented, I took a few steps backward, nearly tripping as I collided with another body. I turned to see Miles and, next to him, a girl in a duster coat with long blond hair spilling from underneath a knit cap.

"Kathryn! There you are," he said. "I've been looking everywhere for you."

But the way he stood with his hands to the fire told me he might have forgotten I was supposed to even be there in the first place.

"I'm Anna," said the girl in the duster. She held a gloved hand out for me to shake.

"Anna's here studying abroad," Miles told me. "From Stockholm. She's staying with my uncle in Minneapolis."

"Oh . . . ," I said. "Fascinating." Miles hadn't told me he was bringing somebody else.

Anna nodded, I nodded, and Miles slipped his hand into the pocket of my peacoat, twining his fingers with mine. Chloe and Dina called this "dating"; all I knew was that it got more confusing the longer I tried to keep it up.

I untangled my fingers so I could take another drink from Chloe's thermos. Warm numbness now worked its way through my body, replacing confusion with a strange and delicious inability to care. People around us were singing, so I started singing, too. Somebody I didn't know put her arm around me, and we swayed back and forth to music that blared out of one of the parked cars. Chloe laughed, chasing sparks from the fire, and I laughed, too. I couldn't help myself. I felt silly and invincible and gloriously, deliriously free.

"I have to go to the bathroom," I said to Miles. "Where do I do that?"

He peered over the crowd, toward where the trees gathered into darkness. I followed his gaze and understood: Peeing was going to be an adventure.

I left them and set off, past groups of partiers, picnic tables, and drums overflowing with garbage. As I got closer, a group of guys stumbled past. Somewhere in the drowning part of me that still worried about practicalities, I hoped they weren't headed for the same patch of trees I had targeted; I didn't want to have to find some other place to go.

"Because it's there!" one of the guys kept shouting. "Because it's there!"

Chloe rushed up with several others who appeared to be following the guys. "Jason Riley's going to climb down the rocks," she told me. "He's insane!"

I veered off and chose another spot to enter the woods. Picking my way through branches and brush, I stopped just in time to keep from plunging over a cliff.

A vista lay in front of me, lit by the full moon. Below and out as far as I could see was the lake and, at my feet, a steep drop-off with boulders frozen in a tumble, one over the other until they reached some unseeable bottom.

This was why they called it The Rocks.

I stepped to the edge of a long, smooth rock, letting cold air fill my lungs. Could I have dreamed, when I got that pink invitation to Brooke's slumber party, that in just a couple of months I would be in this strange place, partying with the most powerful people at school? Who was I? What was I turning into? If I took one more step, could I fly?

I slid my foot backward, moving away from the ledge. I was starting to scare myself. Squatting over a pile of leaves, I quickly emptied my bladder, and then I went to find Brooke.

As I walked back toward the party, I heard a familiar laugh coming from a cluster of picnic tables not far from the bonfire. Brooke sat on one of them with a group of girls who wore swimming letters on their jackets. She had a cup in her hand, and when I sat down next to her I could definitely smell beer.

"You're drunk," she said. "I told you to be careful."

"It's hard being careful." I put my head on her shoulder. "I tried."

My vision had narrowed to a tiny rectangle in my lap. A hand thrust in, offering another shot of whiskey, and my hand rose instinctively to accept it.

"She's had enough," Brooke told the owner of the hand. "Thanks."

"You sound like my mother," I said.

"Your mother is awesome. I love your mother."

I lifted my head, then put my feet to the ground and stood up. The movement widened my perspective and I felt as if I could step outside my body for a minute to see—really see—myself. There I stood, my clothes rumpled, my head lolling as I swayed back and forth, trying to keep focused.

"I'm sorry, Brooke," I said. "I think you might be mad at me."

"I'm not mad at you." She fiddled with the zipper of her coat. I couldn't tell if she meant it or not.

"You really are my best friend. You know that?"

"Uh-oh, careful," said one of the swimmers. "She's got the 'I love you, man's.'"

"I don't have the anything, mans." I grabbed Brooke's hand; suddenly this was the most important thing in the world. "You are a great singer," I told her. "You are a great person. And I hope you know how much I appreciate everything you've ever done for me, Brooke. Really!"

For the first time in weeks, I saw a smile play about the corners of her mouth; this time I felt almost positive it was genuine.

"You're a mess," she said.

"I know. I'm an idiot. About so many things."

A scream rose from beyond the bonfire. Neither of us paid attention. People screamed a lot at parties, I figured; somebody had probably snuck up on somebody, or someone had spilled beer down someone else's back. I didn't pay attention because, for the first time in what seemed like weeks, Brooke wasn't acting angry or defensive or shut down.

"Where's Miles?" she asked me.

I sighed, feeling something inside of me crumble. I'd been dying to talk with her about this, and maybe now she would let me.

"Miles is making me insane."

Her face hardened. "Insane how?"

The alcohol made it hard for me to get the problem into words. "Well, like tonight," I said. "Did you see him here with Ahnn-na?" I drew the name out for dramatic effect.

"I saw him," she said, her eyes narrowing. "Anna's from a foreign country. He can't just leave her alone out here when she doesn't know anybody."

I could feel our moment slipping away. I panicked, trying to get it back.

"I know! It's just . . ." I could not think of a way to make what I wanted to say sound right. "It's just . . . Miles is . . . not as great as everybody thinks."

Brooke reared back in surprise.

"What? Is he not paying enough attention to you or something?"

"Sort of . . ." When you put it like that, it really did sound petty, and I could tell from the way her eyebrow stayed glued to the top of her forehead that petty was exactly how she had taken it. I opened my mouth to try to explain again but there came another scream, this time too loud to ignore, especially when news began to ripple through the crowd that something bad had happened.

Nick Zimmerman strode past us with his car keys out.

"The cops are coming," he said. "Riley fell down the fucking ravine."

Another guy ran past us, blubbering. "Man, I think he's dead down there. We haven't heard anything in, like, twenty minutes."

"Shit," said Brooke. She dumped her beer, got up from the table, and scanned the clearing. She started grabbing people as they ran by, asking, "Where's Bill Dempsey? Have you seen Brice?"

I stood frozen, the alcohol still buzzing in my brain, wondering what it meant. Would we be caught? Would we all get arrested? What would I tell my parents? I couldn't find anybody I recognized in the roiling, panicked crowd.

Then I saw a duster coat and long blond hair.

"Miles!" I shouted. "Miles!"

Miles dropped his arm from Anna's shoulder as he turned, looking guilty even in the midst of such chaos, and the word I had been hunting for earlier came to me: *Miles is a player. Matt was right.*

But Miles could have been an ax murderer for all I cared at that moment. I ran up to him, panting. "We have

to go. We need a ride. You have to take everybody home!"

Miles grabbed Anna's hand and headed for the parking lot while I trailed behind. "Wait a minute," I shouted. I broke away and ran back toward the bonfire. "We need to get Brooke and Chloe. They can't find Bill and Brice. Miles, we have to wait!"

But when I looked, I couldn't find Brooke anywhere.

Jason Riley, it turned out, didn't die. He didn't even get hurt very badly, just some cuts and scrapes from sliding down the rocks and getting caught in a tree, where he waited until a firefighter could rappel down for him under the glare of floodlights from a massive pumper truck. Chloe had the whole story when Dina and I met her the next day at the mall.

"They're going to make him pay for the equipment and the firefighters' time," she said, stirring her Frappuccino at the food court. "He's so screwed."

The bags at her feet rattled as she shifted in her chair. Only one of them was mine, a pair of shoes I'd found on sale to go with the Homecoming gown my mother was making. I'd hidden that fact from Chloe and Dina by pretending not to find anything I liked in any of the stores we visited. "There's nothing wrong with being picky," Chloe had said as I tried on, and then rejected, dresses so beautiful they made my teeth hurt. I couldn't help wondering whether she would have said the same thing about being poor.

"So who got caught?" Dina asked. "I heard, like, a hundred people went to jail."

"Nobody went to jail," Chloe sniffed. "Nick told me they were taking names, but there were so many people they had to quit after fifty or so. We got stuck in this huge traffic jam trying to drive away, and the cops started going car to car. Bill and Brice made Brooke drive since she only had a couple beers, and she was a mess because she doesn't have her license, and we hit the highway ramp just in time because this policeman was only, like, four cars back. I was pissing my pants. You have no idea."

Dina turned to me. "And you made the getaway with Miles. How was the after-party?"

I shrugged, staring into my plain black coffee. "I think Miles and I are over. He brought somebody else and she was all over him the entire way home."

"Anna the Swedish snow bunny," said Chloe, nodding. "Word has it he already asked her to Homecoming. Sorry, Kathryn."

"It was nice of him to tell me," I muttered. "Especially now that I've got a dress and shoes."

"Don't worry." Chloe gave a dismissive wave. "I'll set you up with somebody better." Her cell phone rang and her lips turned up as she checked the screen. "It's Brooke."

I sat forward; I'd been trying to reach Brooke all morning.

"Hey, B," Chloe said. "So what happened after I left last night? Was it depraved and hilarious, and will we get to see it on YouTube?"

Chloe's smile faded while she listened. She eyed me, and then handed over the phone.

"Where are you?" Brooke sounded angry.

"At the mall," I said. "I've been trying to call you."

"I slept in. Why aren't you here? We were going to Hildy's recital. Remember?"

I dropped my head into my hand, rubbing my temple as an old conversation came back to me. Brooke and I had talked about hearing her voice teacher's studio perform; I must have mixed up the dates.

"I'm sorry," I said. "We never discussed it again. I guess I was thinking it was next month."

Silence. I shook my head, staring at the bags on the floor. What did she want me to say? It was an innocent mistake, and if she hadn't been ignoring her phone all morning, then I wouldn't have made it in the first place. Chloe wrote something on a napkin and shoved it under my nose. *Tell her to come out. Dollar movie at four.*

"Why don't you come here?" I said. "We were thinking of seeing a movie."

"I'm not going to the movies. I told Hildy I'd be at her recital."

"Look," I said. "I'm sorry. I can get over there in twenty minutes if you wait."

"Just forget it."

There it was again, that voice that heaped guilt at my feet, then shut me out. Nothing I did seemed to be good enough for Brooke anymore, unless it was sitting at her piano talking about opera. "Do you want me there or not?" I said. In the background I could hear the bell warning theatergoers to take their seats.

"It's starting," she said. "I have to go." The line went dead, so fast that I wondered if I'd been hung up on.

"Well?" said Chloe. "Is she coming?"

"No," I said, confused and annoyed all at the same time. "She seems upset."

Chloe shrugged. "She gets like that. Her dad's probably not returning her calls again."

"Yeah," said Dina. "Whenever he gets a new job he goes incommunicado."

I shook my head. "I don't think that's it. Her dad's not even working right now. She told me he's in Romania with Jake."

Chloe tilted her head. "Where?"

"Romania. You know, on the new *Mephistopheles* movie?"

Chloe and Dina looked at each other, then they looked at me again, their eyes big as volleyballs.

"Hold on," said Chloe. "Did you just say *Mephistopheles*? And *Jake*? Are you telling us Brooke's dad is in Romania with *Jake Jaspers*?"

"*The* Jake Jaspers?" said Dina. "As in the movie star?"

They looked at each other once more and started to giggle nervously.

"No way!" Dina sputtered. "Oh my God!"

Chloe reached across the table and grabbed me by the arm. "You're kidding, right? How do you know?"

"I thought everybody knew." I faltered. "Her dad's gay. Is that a big deal or something?"

Chloe gaped at me like I'd just suggested she wear last year's fashion. "No, that's not a big deal. Everybody knows Brooke's dad is gay."

"But he's going out with Jake Jaspers?" Dina squealed. "Oh my God, you have to tell us everything!"

My thoughts raced in a million different directions as I scrambled to piece together what this meant. Brooke had never told me her dad's relationship was a secret, but apparently it was so big that she hadn't even told Chloe. That realization brought a bigger, far more heady one:

I was closer to Brooke Dempsey than the most popular girls in my class.

I should have stopped right there. I should have said that I'd made it all up or misunderstood or even that I'd promised Brooke I wouldn't tell, but Chloe and Dina were clinging to my every word. The spotlight was on me but instead of shrinking away, for once I let it flood me with power.

I took a deep breath and told them everything.

They listened, breaking in every now and then with a "Holy shit!" or a "No way!" and I don't think it was Jake Jaspers that interested them so much as the fact that there was something about Brooke they didn't know.

Chloe actually seemed angry about it.

"Brooke and I have been best friends since sixth grade," she said. "How come she told you all that and not me?"

"I don't know," I said, and squirmed in my seat. The spotlight had become too bright; now that I'd told her Brooke's secret I couldn't take it back.

"Seriously," she went on. "What kind of person doesn't tell their best friend something like that?"

Now, when I think back on it, I realize there's another question she should have asked; or maybe I should have asked it of myself: *What kind of person tells other people her best friend's secrets?*

But I didn't ask that question. If I had, it could have changed everything.

"Do *you* know where she is?" Chloe asked me as she peered up at the crowded stadium. The Homecoming game had just started, and we'd settled near the bottom row, underneath a blanket with Chloe's date, Mitch, and an empty seat where my date, Owen Lynch, was supposed to be. I shook my head no.

"Maybe she's pissed she doesn't have a date," Chloe said. "I tried setting her up with Sam Langenkamp but she acted like he had a disease or something. If Brooke wants to be picky that's her call. But people expect to see her at an event like this, you know?"

I nodded, though secretly I was glad Brooke wasn't there. I was fed up with the guilt trips, the silent treatments, the way she'd want to be around me one minute, then turn around the next and act as if I'd disappointed her in some profound and secret way. I wanted to enjoy my first real Homecoming, to sit in the elite seats at the stadium, then drink in the romance of the dance and let myself go at the after-party without feeling bad.

I glanced around, looking for Owen. He'd left to talk with some of his wrestling buddies, and I hoped I didn't look like a third wheel sitting alone while Chloe and Mitch shared a cup of hot chocolate. Not that a date really mattered; to me, Owen seemed more like a prop—a movie character who fades into the background of a bigger, more epic scene. The lights, the band, the cheerleaders, the other A-listers who sat around us like royalty—they were amazing.

And I was a part of it.

Chloe put her hand on my arm, pulling me out of my seat.

"I hate football," she said to Mitch. "We're going to the bathroom."

I put my foot forward and felt the toe of my boot sink into something soft. A howl of pain sent me back onto my rear end; the guy on the bleacher directly in front of me started rocking back and forth, fingers in his mouth.

"Oh my God!" I stooped to offer help, though I had no idea what to do. "Are you okay? I'm so sorry!"

He examined his smashed fingers, and while he did I got a chance to study him: He had shaggy brown hair and eyes that managed to look kind even while they gazed back up at me in agony.

"Kathryn," Chloe said, as smooth as ever. "If you're going to stomp on people's hands, at least be polite and tell them who you are."

"Um . . . Chloe just said it. I'm Kathryn." I held out my hand, blushing. He went to reciprocate, realized he was offering his injured one, and gave me the other to shake instead.

"Let me get you some ice," I said.

He laughed. "It's ten below out. If I want ice I'll just leave my gloves off."

"Then at least let me buy you a hot chocolate. You've got to let me make it up to you."

"How about a dance later on?"

Those words started a somersault in my stomach. All of that time I'd spent wondering and worrying about Miles—why hadn't I considered that there were other guys at school, guys just as good-looking, who wouldn't treat me like just another member of the harem?

I told him I had a date. "Boodawg's then," he said. "Promise you'll find me at the party?"

"Okay," I said, blushing even deeper.

"Alex Kelly," Chloe told me as we walked up the steps toward the restrooms on the concourse level. "Class: senior. Status: single."

Later at the dance, I watched Alex swaying with Angela Van Zant across the gym. He lifted his fingers in a miniature wave as Owen draped himself over me, running his hands up and down my back and singing in my ear.

When we got to Bud's house, I left Owen at the door and started looking for Alex. It really was like some sort of movie. People in suits and gowns mingled in the dim rooms, their faces illuminated by firelight and the glow from a few strategically placed lamps. The dramatic lighting transformed my hand-sewn dress into a designer gown. Venturing into the kitchen, I filled a delicate-stemmed glass with wine and savored the first sips.

That's when I saw her: Brooke, sitting in the breakfast

nook with her brothers, wearing jeans and a Baldwin sweatshirt. I waved; she didn't wave back. I tried again. Nothing.

"Great," I muttered. "What's wrong now?"

Chloe walked past, and I snatched her hand. "Brooke's here," I said.

"Where?" Chloe craned her neck and I pulled her out the kitchen door, onto the heated patio; I didn't want Brooke to see us talking about her.

"She's in the kitchen with Bill and Brice. She looks angry."

"Really?" Chloe stepped over to a window and peeked in. "She looks like she always does. I bet she's just regretting she wore that tragic sweatshirt out of the house."

I peeked over Chloe's shoulder just as Brooke turned toward us. I ducked, bringing Chloe down with me.

"Watch your wine!" she said, pulling back as the red splashed dangerously close to her dress.

"Sorry." I took a gulp to reduce the chances of an overflow. "It's just that I keep getting the impression she's mad at me, and I'm starting to wonder if maybe something might have happened."

"What could have happened?"

"I don't know. Did she tell you anything?"

"No." Chloe stood back up, smoothing her skirt and looking annoyed. "I'm sure it's nothing beyond the fact

that she's missed out on most of the night already. Don't worry about it. I know Brooke better than anybody else and she's moody. That's all. Whatever it is, she'll get over it."

But I knew it was more than that; I knew, because there was no way I could *not* know. Every time I turned around I saw Brooke glaring at me. The glamorous movie had turned into a horror show.

"Wow. You look amazing." I'd just ducked into the study when Alex Kelly appeared next to me, a cocktail glass in each hand. "Gin and tonic?" he said, holding one of them out to me. "It's good gin. You'll barely taste it."

I slouched against the mahogany desk, grateful for the distraction. "Thanks," I told him. "I needed this." The drink was sweet with a hint of bitterness at the end; after a few sips, a thrumming started in my ears that harmonized nicely with the cozy blur from the wine.

As if on cue, Brooke walked in through a door half hidden by a massive fern. I sipped hard on the tiny straw in my drink.

"Look," said Alex. "I'm not out to make enemies, especially not with a guy like Owen Lynch. But I don't want you leaving tonight without giving me your phone number, okay?"

My entire body flooded with warmth, and for a moment Brooke disappeared from my thoughts. What-

ever was wrong between the two of us, nothing could spoil the beautiful, kind way that Alex looked at me just then. I opened the desk drawer and found a box of Sharpies inside.

"Here," I said, holding out my hand. I wrote my number on the back of his, next to the shadow of a bruise where my boot had pressed his knuckles. "Careful you don't wash that off now."

"You don't have to worry," he said. "I'll be calling way before that even becomes an issue."

He kept his hand in mine a second longer before slipping away, across the room and right past Brooke, who looked after him, then back at me.

I became aware of it then: waves of energy. The anger coming off of her was so strong I could actually feel it, and in that moment I knew the truth:

Brooke Dempsey hated me.

BROOKE

"YOU'RE PLOTTING MURDER, AREN'T YOU, Brookie?" Bill Jr. leaned up against Boodawg's study door with a half-empty beer in his hand. "You look . . ." He gave me a twice-over, trying to find some way of describing me in jeans and a sweatshirt when everybody else was in sport coats and gowns.

"Like an Amazon?" I snapped.

"Not quite what I was going for."

"It's what you would have come up with if I had heels on."

"Okay . . ." He smiled uneasily. "Look. I know you're upset, but try letting it go for a while, huh?"

He could have been talking about the whole semester. About my entire stupid life up to that point. But he wasn't. He was talking about the voice mail I'd gotten on my way out the door for the game.

"Hey, Brookie, it's Dad. Look, you're going to be getting a note from Jake's publicist. I think you met Marina last summer in L.A. Anyway I'm calling because I want to make sure you read her message and do what she says. I know you probably had nothing to do with this mess but it's important, so make sure the twins see it, too. All right, honey? I love you."

I went back to my room, checked my email, and sure enough, there was something from marina@ jamesassociates.com in my inbox.

Dear Friend:

You are receiving this message because Jake Jaspers has identified you as a friend or family member in a position to know about his relationship with Mr. William Dempsey. You likely also know that, for various reasons, Mr. Jaspers and Mr. Dempsey have taken steps to avoid making their relationship known to the public at large. I am writing today to inform you that, over the past week, messages have appeared on the websites http://celebsightings.com and http://gossipmonger.net from persons claiming to have knowledge of Mr. Jaspers's relationship with Mr. Dempsey. While rumors are a fact of life for a personality such as Mr. Jaspers and while little can be done to keep people from speculating if they so choose, the frequency of these messages and the nature of the information they contained has caused us some concern. I have contacted the administrators of these sites, and the offending posts have been taken down. I do not think any lasting damage has been done. I am writing simply to remind you of the delicate circumstances surrounding Mr. Jaspers's personal life and to ask that you refrain from any conversations or activities that might expose him to scrutiny. I am certain that these recent incidents were misunderstandings, and I trust that you share my commitment to respecting Mr. Jaspers's wishes where his personal affairs are concerned.

Best,

Marina James

I went to the sites Marina had listed. The posts about Jake weren't up, but there were posts about other celebrities. They were disgusting and mean. Nobody I knew would put up something like that about my dad. Nobody I knew *knew* enough about Dad and Jake.

Except for one person.

"It's my fault," I told Bill.

"It's not your fault."

"But I told . . ." I could barely say her name, I was so furious.

Bill shook his head. "Anybody could have done it. If Dad wants to play boyfriends of the rich and famous he has to expect stuff like this."

My skin started to crawl. Bill and Brice had forgotten about Dad the second he moved out of our apartment in New York. They'd made a new life in Lake Champion like it was where we'd belonged all the time, and they'd bought the whole Midwestern party boy thing hook, line, and sinker. They couldn't even stay at college—they had to keep coming back and hanging out with the high school kids.

Pathetic.

"I should have known you wouldn't care," I said.

"It doesn't matter if I care or not," Bill told me. "Dad'll be all right, Brooke. Just like always. You already missed the game and the dance because of this. Can't you try to have some fun?"

No. I couldn't. Across the room I could see Kathryn in her strapless purple dress, sucking on a gin and tonic. Would she *really* do something that horrible? I hadn't told anybody else about Dad. And she'd changed so much since we'd first started hanging out.

Or maybe I'd never really known her at all.

I started to circle.

Wherever she went, I followed. I watched her do her ice-queen act with Owen Lynch. I watched her flirt with

Alex Kelly. I watched her down a glass of wine. Then a beer. Then more gin. The more I watched, the more pissed off I got. Kathryn was shallow and fake and sloppy, just like everybody else. She had her perfect little family—her dad who mowed the lawn and her mom who made birthday pot roasts. Who was she to mess with mine?

"Hey, B." Chloe popped up in the living room. "What're you doing?"

"Looking at a two-faced bitch," I said.

Chloe looked where I was looking. Her smile disappeared. "Kathryn? What did Kathryn do?"

I shook my head. I couldn't tell her. That would mean telling things I didn't want anybody else to know—things I shouldn't have told anybody, *ever*. So I settled for, "What *didn't* Kathryn do? She's a liar and a backstabber. That good enough?"

Chloe looked worried. "I thought you liked Kathryn."

"Yeah, well, you thought a lot of things." Kathryn headed out to the patio, and I followed, stepping around the couch and leaving Chloe standing alone.

When I found Kathryn again she was laughing like an idiot at one of Tim McNamara's stupid jokes. She looked over at me, and the blackness just went everywhere. Kathryn wanted to be an A-lister. She wanted to date all the best guys and go to the best parties. She thought because she was beautiful and little that she could steal my friends and step all over people to get what she wanted. Well, I was the top of the A-list. I was the one with the power. And I decided it was time.

Time to take care of Kathryn.

I waited for Tim to move, then I walked past, bumping her with my shoulder. We hit so hard her drink sloshed onto her shoes.

"Hey!" She laughed. "Watch where you're going, B."

I bumped her again. This time, her plastic cup bounced to the concrete. She shook her hands, trying to get the beer off them. I leaned over so I could whisper into her ear.

"You are a bitch. I know what you did, and if you know what's good for you, you will watch yourself."

She backed up, staring at me with those big, wide eyes. "What?" she said. "What are you talking about?"

I kept my voice down—I didn't need the whole school hearing what I had to say, but I made sure that she could hear every word.

"You know exactly what I'm talking about. You are a bitch and a liar and a backstabber. And you're lucky I don't kick your ass right here."

There. I'd said just enough to put her in her place. I started to walk away, but Kathryn rushed ahead and planted herself in front of the kitchen door.

"No." She stuck her chest out. Her eyes held on to mine with those gold flecks flashing. "You're not doing this again, Brooke," she said. "If you've got a problem, you can tell me what it is."

"Unbelievable." I tried to get past her, putting my weight into one giant shove. She held steady. This time, it was me who had to step backward.

"I know you're mad," she said. "You've been mad at me for weeks, and I'm through trying to guess why." She put her arms up on either side of the door. "This is it. Whatever is wrong, we are going to talk about it. Now."

KATHRYN

BROOKE LOOKED AT ME LIKE a boxer sizing up an opponent on the opposite side of a ring. I waited, half terrified, but also strangely relieved. At least I would finally know why she hated me so much.

Chloe and Dina rushed out of the house, stopping when they saw us.

"Hey," Chloe said. "What's going on?"

Brooke scowled at me. "You put that shit online about my dad."

Online? I felt my jaw drop, my brow knit together in confusion.

"I did *what*?"

"You went online about my dad and Jake. You knew it was private, and you posted it for the whole world to read."

"I did not," I said. "I didn't tell anyone. . . ."

But suddenly, I felt sick. The conversation at the mall

came back to me, the one after the Senior Keg, and the horrible truth of what I had done—or helped somebody else do—hit like a knee to the stomach.

"It must have been Chloe or Dina," I blurted out. "One of them must have done it!"

"Excuse me?" Chloe whirled around and glared at me. "Thanks a lot, Kathryn. Don't drag us into your crap."

"We're not the ones who are P-O-O-R," Dina sneered. "How much did they give you for all the details, Kathryn?"

There they stood, two girls who had been my friends just minutes earlier, eyeing me now like an unwelcome stranger. Chloe, who always seemed to have a solution for every awkward situation, offered no aid whatsoever.

"You have to believe me," I pleaded with Brooke. "I didn't tell anybody but Chloe and Dina!"

Brooke scowled even deeper. "You weren't supposed to tell *anybody*."

"I know that now, and I'm sorry. But I wouldn't do something like post it online. I would never do something like that."

Brooke stepped toward me, pushing Chloe out of the way. "Do you ever drop the act?" she asked.

"What act?"

"The one you're doing right now. Where you treat people like shit and then pretend you're just poor, confused little Kathryn."

"But I don't get it. Who have I treated like shit?"

"Me, for one." She thrust out her hand and started ticking off her fingers. "Your parents, who you totally disrespect. And what about Miles? You have no idea how lucky you were to have him, but all you could do was bitch."

I'm sure it was the alcohol, making certain things clear and other things, like my judgment, hopelessly blurry, but I realized then something I should have picked up on from the start: The way Brooke had made herself scarce when Miles started asking me out, the way she'd turned sullen when I'd tried to talk about him . . .

"*You* like Miles!" I said, nearly shouting because it was so obvious, and I had been so stupid not to see it sooner.

Chloe gasped and Brooke shrank back, her eyes darting frantically around to see if anybody else had heard me.

"It's true!" I went on. "You like him. Why didn't you tell me?"

Brooke looked like she might be about to cry. "I shouldn't have had to tell you," she hissed; the expression on her face begged me to keep my voice down.

No, I thought. *No. I won't be quiet.* So much could have been avoided with just a few honest words, and now it was too late. I moved forward, emboldened by the alcohol.

"I don't read minds, Brooke. I asked you for weeks what was wrong, and you told me nothing. I'm starting to think maybe *I'm* the one who's been treated like shit."

"I didn't tell you because I didn't think I could trust you," she said. "And I was right. You're a fake and a crappy drunk and you're making a fool out of yourself."

I'd had enough alcohol to make me buzzed, but not so much that I couldn't quickly scan back through the evening and take stock of my actions; I'd done nothing out of line, so what could Brooke—Brooke, who, according to Chloe, had thrown up at a Steak 'n' Shake and bared her behind on more than one occasion—be talking about?

"So you're the only one who gets to drink and be stupid and have fun?" I asked. "How in the world is that fair?"

"I'm not going to talk about this," she said.

"Why? Is it too embarrassing? I heard about all the things you've done when you were wasted, and unless my memory is faulty I don't think *I've* ever vomited in public, nor have I ever run around with my pants down. So tell me, Brooke, just what makes you think you're any better than me?"

Rocking forward, she pushed up the sleeves of her

sweatshirt. "You really want to know?"

"Yes, Brooke. I really want to know."

"Fine," she said. "I'll tell you. I am better because *I* don't take everything for granted. Music? You're lucky you're so good because otherwise you'd be nothing but a hack. Matt . . . Where is he tonight? Sitting at home watching movies by himself?"

That one hurt, because she was right; hours earlier, when I'd gone by his house to check in, I'd found Matt with the *Star Wars* series on DVD, watching alone in the dark while Anakin Skywalker fumed over an imagined betrayal by his best friend and mentor. He'd tried to get me to stay for the end of the movie, but I told him I had to go—I didn't want to be late for my date.

"Leave Matt out of this," I snapped. "Matt's fine. He understands."

"What? That you're a two-faced popularity whore who drops her real friends as soon as someone shinier comes along?"

A crowd had started to gather, drawn by the rising volume of our voices. One of Brooke's brothers emerged from the group, saying, "Hey, hey. What's this all about, now?" Brice put one hand on my shoulder, the other on Brooke's, attempting to separate us. I shook him off.

"You picked me," I said. "Remember?"

Brooke laughed. "My mistake. You're nothing special.

You think you are, but just watch how fast I can take it all away."

"God, who are you?" I said. We had moved beyond petty misunderstandings to somewhere darker, a place I didn't want to go but couldn't resist. "*What* are you? Is this some kind of high school mafia movie? Are you like the Douglas High Godfather?"

"I might as well be, as far as you're concerned," she said. "The only reason you're here tonight—the only reason you are *anywhere*—is because of me."

"And *you're* only here because of your brothers."

She stopped, eyes gaping, red blotches beginning to show on her cheeks. I knew I'd struck close; all I needed was to push a little further and I would find my mark.

"Look at yourself, Brooke. You have everything, and yet all *you* can talk about is how much you want to get away. It's like you think you're doing us a big favor by allowing us to bask in your presence. You're the Queen B because you've had somebody telling you that ever since you were old enough to put on a show, but that's all this is—a show. You're Daddy's Little Star, and damn, don't you believe it?"

I didn't see her fist coming, but I felt the blow, like a hammer to my left eye socket. It sent me backward, onto my rear end, and then flat onto the floor. The alcohol kept my eye from hurting; it also kept me on the ground. I remember lying there with my hand to my cheek, moaning, "What happened? What happened?" And then everything went black.

For the first couple of days afterward, nothing happened; in fact, I woke up the next morning certain that the fight had been a dream. Then I looked into my bathroom mirror, and there it was—the purple welt under my eye. I hurried to cover it with makeup, trying to hide the mark from my parents but also hoping that, by concealing it, I could somehow make the entire, awful evening go away.

Monday at school, nobody talked to or looked at me. I walked around in an odd, shocked calm while people tried to make sense of what had happened and figure out which side to take. Then, on Wednesday, it started. A group of seniors sat giggling at the back of the choir room, huddled over their BlackBerrys as I came in after lunch. When they saw me they started to whisper. Brooke walked in and they gave her high fives, then they looked back at me and doubled over laughing. Brooke shot one icy glare in my direction, then gathered her folder and went to her seat. That night Matt needed just a few minutes of cybersleuthing to find what they were laughing at: a clip of Brooke punching me that someone had taken with their cell phone and posted on YouTube. Over and over, her fist flew into my face and I staggered backward. I looked so small next to her, so awkward and exposed, that I had a hard time believing it was really me.

The next morning my locker was egged. The weary-looking janitor made me clean the mess myself, and when our principal, Ms. Van Whye, came by to ask who'd done it, I couldn't tell the truth; I told her it was a prank by some friends who were getting back at me for a prank I'd played on them, and she threatened me with detention.

I still held out hope, though—if only I could talk with Chloe. I found her during morning break, with Dina at the A-list bench in the commons.

"Hey, guys," I said, hurrying over. "What's up?"

"So I'm thinking a Marie Antoinette theme for prom," Chloe was saying to Dina. "I'm the first junior to ever head up the planning committee and I want to make a splash."

"That'd be so sweet!" Dina squealed.

"Hey," I tried again. "I loved that movie. I could hel—"

"Or maybe not Marie Antoinette. What about black and white? Like a debutante ball. Check out these pics I got online."

Chloe whipped out her cell phone and, wedging me out, leaned over to show Dina the screen. My ears burned and my breath came short as I backed away, hoping no one had seen them ignore me.

I spent the weekend fielding hang-up phone calls and obscene IMs, returning to school to find the worst humiliation yet: Alex Kelly, waiting for me at my locker. For a moment I allowed myself to hope that maybe—just maybe—he'd come to pick up where we'd left off in those final moments at Bud's party, but when I got close enough to see into those kind brown eyes, I found them instead filled with pity and disgust.

"Leave me alone," he said.

"Excuse me?" I paused with my backpack half off my shoulder. I hadn't spoken to Alex since the party, so how much more alone could I leave him?

"You heard me," he repeated. "Leave me alone. Stop calling. Stop emailing. Stop leaving notes in my locker."

"I didn't leave anything in your locker."

"You're telling me this isn't from you?"

He held out a piece of notebook paper, folded in quarters with a broken heart seal. I opened it to find an uncanny imitation of my handwriting.

Alex. Please. I can't stop thinking about you. When are you going to call me? When are we going to go out? I think I'm in love with you. Please don't ignore me.
Kathryn

My cheeks were on fire and my stomach churned; someone had been pretending to be me, begging Alex for attention, and he had believed it; he thought I was some sort of pathetic, needy stalker.

"We're not going out," he said, taking the note back and crumpling it in his fist. "I don't like you. Okay? I don't."

I stood in front of him, searching through the shame for something to say, while underneath it another emotion began to blossom. I had made so many mistakes—believing Brooke when she told me nothing was the matter; believing Chloe when she said she would keep Brooke's secret; believing my newfound popularity was real and not an illusion that would shatter as soon as Brooke decided to end our friendship with her fist. I had betrayed Matt, I'd betrayed Brooke, and I'd betrayed my parents, who'd gotten a call just days earlier from the school counselor, concerned about how badly my midquarter grades had fallen.

"How could you do this?" my mother had asked when she'd gotten off the phone. "You know how important your schoolwork is."

Yes, I had made mistakes—terrible ones; but did I deserve this?

I straightened, willing myself to look at Alex, if only for a second. "You couldn't wait to be with me when you thought I was with Owen Lynch."

I saw his features soften, like he knew that what I'd said was true. Almost as quickly, they hardened again.

"You aren't who I thought you were then."

"You're right," I said. Then I turned and ran out of the building and away from school, to the Mexican restaurant where I waited for Matt to come and find me like I always knew he would.

"Ignore them," he told me over my fifth Dr Pepper. "Sooner or later they'll stop."

I learned to keep my head down, keep moving, keep from making eye contact—let people do what they were going to do and hope it would be over quickly because any other reaction would just invite more torment. I buried myself in my schoolwork, in music, in Matt, and he was right; gradually they did stop. Torment turned to cold shoulders and then to blank stares, which were even more painful because before when I was invisible, it was only because nobody knew me. Now, everybody knew who I was, and they knew—because Brooke had told them—that I wasn't worth so much as a second glance.

In a perfect universe I would have forgotten I had ever met Brooke Dempsey. But the box with her black boots greeted me every time I opened my closet door, until finally I took it to the basement and shoved it into the storage room behind the old Christmas decorations. And then, there was choir. Every day Brooke stood in the back row, just nine spots away, showing me nothing but that regal profile. But I could tell from the energy radiating off of her that she was as painfully aware of me as I was of her. And I knew that whatever had started between us would continue, because music was the one thing neither of us could give up. She could go back to her world, and I could go back to mine, but music was the world in between. As long as we both loved to sing we were destined to meet there, and neither of us would be able to forget.

SENIOR YEAR

*Crescendo: to increase the volume and intensity of
a musical passage*

KATHRYN

"YOU'RE GOING TO HOMECOMING WITH John Moorehouse." The voice comes from behind as I crouch at my locker pulling books into my backpack during morning break. I turn to see Chloe Romelli standing over me.

I should have known this was coming. Ever since John asked me two days ago, questions have been ricocheting around in my head like little boomerangs: *Why did he ask me? Why did I say yes?* And what if John is part of Brooke's new campaign, the bait in some scheme to lure me out so that she and her friends can have a last laugh at my expense? That must be the plan, or Chloe wouldn't be standing here while Laura Lindner, her newest acolyte, glances territorially around the hallway, practically daring somebody to interrupt us.

"He asked me," I say.

"I know he did," Chloe replies. "You going?"

I pause. *Am* I going? I haven't told Matt yet because the whole thing happened so fast, and I wasn't thinking straight thanks to the migraine, which still buzzes faintly behind my eyes. Besides, if this *is* a plot, then I would be an idiot to go walking right into it. John doesn't seem like the type of guy who would participate in one of Brooke's vendettas, but then I don't really know him all that well, now do I?

Still, I hate the tone of voice Chloe is taking with me. Considering that she hasn't given me the time of day in months, I'd say the signs all point to a new plot in the making.

"Well?" she presses. "Are you going or not?"

"Maybe," I say.

"Look." Her voice descends to a concerned-sounding murmur—the same one that used to make me feel like I was being let in on some valuable piece of advice. "Brooke would probably kill me if she knew I was talking to you about this. But I really think you ought to know. She likes John."

She pauses and looks intently at me.

I stare back.

"So?"

Impatience flashes in her eyes; she fixes me with an even weightier stare.

"So maybe you could think about her feelings a little

bit? I don't think she knows about the two of you yet, and that's a good thing, believe me. It's really going to tear her up when she finds out."

This is an interesting twist. After everything that's happened, *I'm* supposed to consider *Brooke's* feelings? I'm so shocked that all I can do is blink.

"Okay?" Chloe says it like we've concluded a nasty bit of business that we can now put behind us. I'm not sure what she thinks we've agreed to, but I am mulling over the information I've just been given: *Brooke likes John.* And John has asked me, the person she hates most in the world, to Homecoming.

"Okay?" Chloe repeats.

"I'll think about it," I say.

"I know you'll make the right decision."

She walks away and Laura scurries after her, past a new Homecoming poster near the language lab door; it's shaped like a dress on a hanger, with "Brooke" written on it in stylish cursive. Her posters are everywhere these days, with their terrible puns—"Dress up your vote: Brooke for Queen!"—and their blurbs about how unfair it is that people with limited funds may be prevented from participating in activities like choir because they can't afford the required uniform.

At lunchtime, I keep one eye over my shoulder while I walk through the music wing to a practice room; if Chloe already knows about John asking me to Homecoming then it's only a matter of time before everybody else at school does, too, and then who knows what will happen? I lock myself in, put my music on the piano stand, and close my eyes, trying to focus. I've been spending lunch hours lately, plus any time that I can steal in the afternoons, in the practice rooms working on my music for the Blackmore. Then I'm back at school from seven to nine most evenings for choir, and by the time I've finished all of my homework I'm barely getting three hours of sleep. Add in the headaches, and I'm starting to get nervous that I might do something stupid—or that I might already have done it by telling John Moorehouse I'll be his date to Homecoming when I know Matt is expecting me to go with him.

Up until now I'd pretty much decided to tell John I changed my mind; somebody like him could easily find someone else to take, and the last thing I want to do is provide entertainment for Brooke and her friends. But something in the way Chloe spoke this morning has been nagging at me. The more I think about it, the more I'm starting to think I've gotten it wrong; maybe John doesn't have an ulterior motive and maybe Brooke *was* hoping he'd ask her instead.

This must have been a twist Chloe didn't anticipate.

And if that's the case, then it may also be my chance

to escape: If I do what Chloe is asking, give up my date with John and let Brooke have him instead, then maybe she'll persuade Brooke to stop with the posters and the water toys. Maybe I can bow out of the Blackmore, too—cobble together the money I need out of an academic honor here, a tiny grant there; Brooke can win the contest and I won't have to worry about her anymore. I feel lighter just thinking about it. I start to retrieve my music from the piano stand, because if I don't compete, then I don't have to practice. But when I pick up my aria book, something falls from between the pages and flutters to the floor. It is a pink slip of paper—an invitation to a slumber party.

I stare at the paper, startled by its sudden reappearance. It lies on the practice room rug, still pristine after sitting a year in my music book. A year ago that invitation was a promise of new friendship; now it's like a glove that a knight would throw down before the final battle in one of Matt's fantasy films. I pick up the invitation and put it into my backpack, then take an apple out of my bag and start to devour it while I head back toward my locker. The commons is filled with people returning from lunch, and just as I pass the big front doors I hear a familiar voice.

"Horndawg, Boodawg," it says. "Potayto, Potahto."

John is making his way up the commons steps with

what appears to be the entire A-list in tow. Chloe, Dina, Bud Dawes, Tim McNamara, even Laura Lindner—they're all together, laughing and sipping soda out of cups from the Chinese restaurant up the street. I pick up my pace, hoping to get past before they can see me, but it's as if John and I are destined to connect; he turns his head just as I duck mine, and our eyes meet.

"Hey, Kathryn, hold up!" The group around him stops, watching with naked interest as John travels the six short steps over to where I'm standing.

"So," he says, a scolding smile on his lips. "I've been hearing some rumors."

I glance over at Chloe, who raises an eyebrow.

"Couldn't this wait until Anatomy?" I whisper.

"What?" he says. "Why are you whispering, and what's with the cloak-and-dagger stuff? Don't tell me those guys were right. You're really backing out of Homecoming?"

He looks genuinely disappointed, and I—I am now genuinely angry. Just what, exactly, does Chloe think I agreed to this morning, and how dare she try to speak for me?

"No," I say. "I mean, I don't want to back out. It's just . . ."

"What? What's it just?"

I am tired and hungry; the apple in my hand wouldn't

have been enough of a meal even if I had been able to finish it before this conversation. I try to stammer out an explanation over the buzzing in my ears, but John is nodding as if he doesn't get or buy any of it, and I know that I haven't managed to utter one coherent sentence because he stops me by waving his hands in front of his face.

"Hold up, hold up!" he says. "This is *way* too complicated. I don't need the history of the world here. All I want to know is are we on or are we off?"

Over his shoulder I can see Chloe staring at me. They are all staring, and I flash back to the night when these same people watched as Brooke's fist slammed me into social oblivion. Suddenly everything comes rushing at me: The Blackmore. My parents and my empty college savings account. The pink invitation.

Brooke.

She likes John.

"We're on," I say loudly, so Chloe will be sure to hear. And as soon as I say it, a manic energy fills my body. There's an odd tingling—an electricity powering me forward as if the answer to all of my problems can be boiled down to this one thing—me going to a dance with the one person nobody would ever expect.

John smiles and says, "Good. See you in class." Then he ambles off to join his friends. I lock eyes with Chloe and then turn to walk back to the practice room to start working on my Blackmore music again.

The rest of the day I can barely sit still. In choir, Brooke's radar is stronger than ever but now, instead of letting it batter me, I stand up straighter, sing louder, and send back my own signal: that I am through being meek little Kathryn, running away from punishments that have gone on for far too long. I am going to stand up and face Brooke.

And I deserve to look good doing it.

In the movies that Matt and I rent, the poor girl gets asked to the dance by the rich guy, and she sews her own dress out of an old gown that her mother wore years ago. But this is real life, and I am tired of being Cinderella, making the most of her rags. When the last bell rings I walk out of school, get into my car, and drive straight to the mall. I've got a paper due for Ms. Amos, a meeting with my Blackmore accompanist, a feature due for the newspaper, and a new Strauss aria to work on, but I don't care. I stride into the most expensive department store and begin filling my arms with the most beautiful dresses I can find. I don't look at price tags; I barely look at the sizes. If something catches my eye, I pull it from the rack and drape it over my arm, creating a rainbow of yellow, lavender, sage green, and blue.

When I can't hold any more, I take the dresses into a

fitting room and start trying them on, beginning with the darkest and working my way toward the whites and creams. The black and the midnight blue are too low cut, the lavender is too frilly, the sky blue and green are much too big.

A rose-colored gown is next. It is floor-length, made of washed silk with grosgrain shoulder straps and a sash that trails its streamers down the back of the skirt. I slip it over my head and let the skirt fall toward my ankles, the satin lining draping cool and graceful against my legs.

"Finding anything you like?" A saleswoman has positioned herself outside my dressing room; I can see her expensive-looking shoes under the curtain.

I gaze at myself in the mirror and see a tired girl transformed. The rose color brings a healthy glow to my skin and sets off my hair, making it look darker and shinier than it really is. I've been losing too much weight, but the dress makes me look willowy instead of emaciated. I can envision myself wearing this gown to Homecoming. I also can see myself wearing it for the Blackmore.

"Miss?" The saleswoman's voice brings me back to practicalities: I'm not onstage yet; I'm standing in a dressing room with my hair in a ponytail and a pair of old black socks on my feet.

"I'm sorry!" I say. "I think I found something. What do you think about this?"

I slide back the curtain, and she clasps her hands together.

"Oh, it's exquisite! Janet Marie, Jillian, come see how beautiful this girl is."

Instantaneously, two other women appear in the fitting area, oohing and aahing over me and my dress. They pull me out of my room and stand me on a white box in front of a three-way mirror. Then they begin pinching and tucking, making adjustments that make the dress fit like it was made just for me, which, according to them, it was. Perhaps they say this to every girl who comes in, or maybe they're buttering me up so they can make a sale—whatever their motivation is, I don't question it because they are making me feel special. It's almost like having my mother here, except she would never come to a place like this, and if she did she'd be too busy worrying about the prices.

"Shoes?" Out of nowhere one of the women produces several pairs of bone-colored heels. There are strappy ones, closed-toed ones, shiny satin ones, and matte fabric ones; I pull off my socks and slip into a pair that have a tiny bow over each toe. Another woman has gone into the store and brought back accessories. Seeing myself in the shoes, the necklace, and the earrings and holding a tiny clutch purse, I feel as if it would be impossible to wear the gown without them; it's only when I take the dress, the shoes, the jewelry, and the clutch to the register that I admit to myself what I've been meaning to do all along. I reach into my purse and take out Matt's credit card number, written on a yellow Post-it from the night when he gave it to me for the Blackmore.

"My dad said I could take his card, but I forgot to get it from him this morning," I tell the clerk. "He gave me the number just now. Can I use it?"

She nods, and I am amazed at how easy it is; the workers here must be used to rich kids running up their parents' credit lines. As I enter the numbers into the electronic keypad I promise that I will tell Matt. Soon, when I've had a chance to make sense of everything.

I use the cover of dusk to sneak my new things into the house and up to my room, where I lay the dress in its garment bag across the floor of my keepsake trunk with the shoes and jewelry on top. Exhaustion bears down on me as I close the lid. The long nights of practicing and studying have finally started to tug me down. With the smell of my mother's spaghetti sauce wafting up from downstairs, I lie on my bed and fall immediately asleep.

Minutes later—it feels like minutes, or maybe it's been an hour—I hear a telephone ringing. Mom tiptoes in, hands me the cordless, then tiptoes back out again.

"Kath?" It's Matt, speaking fast and frantic. "I just got a call from my credit card company. Were you at the mall this afternoon? Somebody was shopping at Goodman's. I told them there was some kind of mistake."

I rise onto my elbow and check my bedside clock. It's six thirty. *Have I missed dinner?* "Um . . ." I run my hand over my face. "I can explain."

"You mean it *was* you? They thought somebody stole my card. They said you got stuff from the lingerie department. . . ."

I feel myself blush; the stockings and garter belt were an impulse buy as I left the store and realized I couldn't wear white cotton panties and L'eggs under such a beautiful dress. I wanted to feel completely remade, totally new, for my stand against Brooke.

Now that I'm talking to Matt about it, though, the romance is draining away, replaced by the realization that I am going to have to tell him the truth.

"It's for Homecoming," I murmur. "I'm sorry, Matt. I was going to tell you. . . ."

"You don't need a new dress, Kath. You'd look beautiful in anything."

I groan; this is going to be more painful than I'd thought. "Matt. I've been wanting to tell you this for a couple of days now."

I pause, hoping maybe he'll say, "Tell me what?" in a

way that lets me know he suspects what's coming. He's quiet, so I go on.

"John Moorehouse asked me to Homecoming. I told him yes, but only because . . ."

"John Moorehouse." He says it like John is some kind of criminal.

"Yes," I say. "But listen to me. Brooke . . ."

"What about our plans?"

I squeeze my eyes shut. "I didn't think we had *plans*, per se. We were just going together because we weren't going with anybody else. Right? I mean that's the way we've done it before, so I thought you wouldn't mind. . . ."

"If you went with John Moorehouse instead of me?"

"Yes." The line goes quiet again, and I panic—the silence is worse than an angry explosion. "Matt . . . are you okay? Please just let me explain."

Matt still doesn't answer; he's begun to piece the whole mess together, to recognize all the terrible layers of what I've done. "So let me get this straight," he finally says. "You're using my money to buy clothes to wear on a date with somebody else? How fucked up is that, Kath?"

My mouth goes dry; he's never spoken to me like this before.

"Listen," I tell him. I swallow hard and then try again. "Brooke will be there. She's planning something and I'm tired of hiding from her."

"So you're going to walk in and invite them all to shit on you again? How do you know John's not in on it, too?"

I think about John's fingers on my temples, the way he understood about school and music, the insecure look when I didn't immediately say yes to his Homecoming invitation. I can't imagine he wants to hurt me, but I have to be honest with Matt—we've always been honest with each other.

"I don't know," I say.

"Look. If you really want to get back at Brooke, then get her at the Blackmore. You're the best singer at school, Kath."

"But *I* am not *music*! I'm not just another contest or award. When I was with Brooke people at least saw that. They saw *me*."

"I see you."

Now it's my turn to be silent.

"But it's not enough," Matt says. "Obviously."

"I'm sorry," I say. I almost offer to return the dress, but I just can't do it. At this moment, it is the one thing giving me a shred of control.

"We could still go to the game together," I offer. "John's playing so he won't be meeting me until afterward."

"Do I look like a complete pussy to you?" His voice is pure venom now. "I'm not going to the game just to get dumped when it's time for the dance to start."

"Matt . . ."

"I want that money back. And I want the hundred dollars for the Blackmore entry, too."

"I'll pay it all," I tell him. "I promise."

"When? It better be soon. If my parents see that I owe this much they'll kick my ass."

"As soon as I can," I say. "By Christmas, I promise."

He is quiet again, and the selfish part of me hopes he will soften and tell me it's all right, that he understands, and that this can be fixed.

But his last words are absolute and unforgiving.

"Enjoy the spotlight, Kathryn. This time, you're going to be there alone."

BROOKE

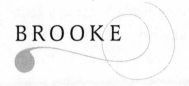

"SO I'M JUST GOING TO tell you this, because I can't believe you don't already know it: John Moorehouse is taking Kathryn Pease to Homecoming."

Chloe peeks at me around the practice room door. From my spot at the piano, she looks like a very concerned decapitated head. It's so weird seeing her in the music wing when she doesn't absolutely have to be here, that I almost wonder if I'm hallucinating.

I must be, because what she just said made absolutely no sense. Kathryn . . . and *John*?

"What?" I say. "When?"

"Since, like, a week ago. While you were off being a loner, everybody's been talking about it."

Slowly the news starts to sink in. As it does, I get a horrible feeling of déjà vu. It's starting again—all that crap from last year. Like somebody pulled the cork out of the bottle of black and let it come gushing back.

I could take care of Kathryn if I wanted to, just like I did then. After that Homecoming punch, people got the message: If they wanted to be friends with me then they couldn't be friends with her. They egged her locker. They ran her off Facebook. They made her into a complete and total leper, and if anybody asked why, I just told them Kathryn had done something bad. I let their imaginations do the rest.

As time went on I convinced myself that she deserved everything she got. I told myself I liked being Queen B and all the power that goes along with it. But now, as the anger and the hurt and the blackness run through my body, I can feel how terrible it is. I'd be lying if I said I didn't enjoy punishing her sometimes. But more than anything else, the past year has just been painful.

I realize now that I'm tired. Tired of hating Kathryn. Tired of caring so damned much. I look up at Chloe and say, "Fine."

"What?" she snaps. "Did you say 'fine'?"

"Yeah." And I mean it even more now. I can still feel the ache of the crush I have on John—the crush I will probably always have. But I also have to be honest. If I had a choice between hanging out with him and working on my music right now, would I do anything different?

No. The truth is no.

"You're not serious," says Chloe. "This is Kathryn

we're talking about. Have you forgotten what she did?"

I can't answer right away. Of course I haven't forgotten. But was it worth a whole year of watching and worrying and wanting to hurt her every single time she walked into the same room as me?

"Oh my God," says Chloe. "Don't tell me you're starting to be friends with her again. Is that what you're trying to tell me?"

I look down at my lap. "I don't know. . . ."

"You can't do this," she says. "Not again."

There are tears in her eyes. Real tears. I've never seen Chloe cry before. "What's that supposed to mean?" I ask.

"It means . . ." She takes a couple of hitching breaths, like she's trying to figure out how to say something important. But then she pulls herself up and her eyes go all hard. "It means Homecoming will be ruined. The King will be dancing with a complete and total nobody!"

"Chloe," I say. "I am going to tell you this to your face so you can't ever come back and say you didn't understand me. Okay?"

She waits while I search for the right words. I love Chloe, but it's time for her to hear the truth.

"I don't care about Homecoming," I tell her. "I could not possibly care less about it. I'm sorry, but that's how I feel."

She sticks her lip out. I can see the little Trump inside

of her holding on with a death grip.

"I don't believe you," she says.

Of course she doesn't. There's only one person who would—just one person who could ever come close to understanding what I've been going through these past few months. Trouble is, the one person who would understand is the one person I can't talk to.

Or can I?

KATHRYN

"HOLD IT UP HIGHER, KATHRYN!" Elise
Cordry hoists the Homecoming Day edition of the *Douglas Picayune* over her head so that passersby can grab it
from her hands. The stadium concourse is packed with
people, so many that we barely have room for our table,
which is stacked with papers containing the foldout
inserts that everybody waves around when the Pirates
make a touchdown. I'm not much for football games, but
when I do go I always like that part—especially when the
game ends and we've won; then everybody rips up the
inserts and throws the pieces into the air so that they
rain down around the stadium like confetti.

If that happens tonight, I won't be out there to see it;
I signed up to work for the paper so I wouldn't have to
sit alone while John is down on the field.

When I first arrived I was so nervous that I thought
I might throw up. Brooke knows I'm going to the dance

with John; I can tell by the way she's been looking at me—right at me, like she can barely keep from coming over and punching me all over again. I can also tell by the snorkels, the CPR manuals, and the SCUBA action figures that have been appearing in and around my locker, faster every day despite my efforts to catch her planting them. I can tell from the anonymous IMs that dog me while I try to do my homework, and the way the A-listers laugh in the hallway when I walk by, not even trying to hide it anymore.

But the excitement inside the stadium tonight is contagious. Elise gives an ecstatic whoop as Tyrone Marshall prances by doing his Captain Jack Sparrow impersonation, and I whoop, too, caught up in the moment. In the stands above our heads, the pep band plays the school fight song; I can hear muffled trumpets and feel the hollow rat-a-tat of the drums. The air smells like popcorn and wood smoke.

Our stack of papers is getting thin and the concourse has filled to capacity; just fifteen minutes remain before the game starts. Transitioning into reporter mode, I fish a pad and pen out of the bag I've stashed under the table and then, before venturing into the crowd, I steel myself by repeating the questions I plan to ask for my postgame reaction story:

"What is your favorite memory of Homecoming?"

And . . .

"How do you think this year compares to last year so far?"

At least I know that, as long as I'm in reporter mode, people will be nice—I have a notebook, and I am going to publish what they say; why would anybody be horrible to someone who's out to make them famous?

"My best memory was last year when I went with my boyfriend, Tom Trooien," Reenie Bezold tells me, flipping her hair as I take down every word. "Now he's at Baldwin and he couldn't come tonight because there's a rush party at his fraternity. I'm going there instead of the dance. So I guess that makes this year better than last year, right?"

"This year kicks last year's ass," says Dennis Dreiling. "Last year we were playing some out-of-conference team called the Gobblers. What kind of dumbass mascot is that?"

Paula Hawk regards me from beneath dyed black bangs and says simply, "Are you really going to the dance with John Moorehouse?"

Paula isn't the only person to ask me this; a few others do, too—mostly the ones who are loners as well. It's as if they think I've accomplished something for everybody else on the fringes. What they don't realize is that the whole thing could be one big joke with me as the punch line. I've been through all of the possibilities already;

I'm even ready for pig's blood, like in Matt's favorite old horror film, though unfortunately I don't have telekinetic powers with which to wreak a fiery revenge on my tormenters.

"My best Homecoming memories? I hope we're making them tonight," says Mr. Lamb, the faculty advisor to the Spirit Committee, as he waxes poetic about the student body coming together with alumni to celebrate the enduring values of friendship, sportsmanship, and school pride.

School pr– I write, and then my pen runs out of ink.

"Hold that thought," I tell him.

Back at the *Picayune* table, Elise rummages through her purse but comes up empty. I dump out my bag but can't find an extra pen.

"I'll be back in a minute," I tell Elise. "I'm going to my locker."

BROOKE

"YOU LOOK AWESOME, BROOKE," CHLOE tells me. "Perfect ten on the dress."

We're in the bathroom under the stadium, working on our hair and makeup. Waiting for the halftime show to start so we can get paraded out on the football field with the rest of the Homecoming court. This bathroom was only made to hold a few people. Not fifty, which is what it feels like with all five Homecoming Queen candidates in here, plus their best friends and Chloe, who's running around spraying hair spray all over the place.

I pull at my dress, trying to get it one more inch over my boobs. When I picked it up from the boutique it ended up being too small. Not so bad that anybody else would notice, but bad enough to make me feel crammed in and overflowing all at the same time. I put on the cashmere shrug. Better. It makes my cleavage less noticeable.

"Wow, that's gorgeous, Brooke," says Angela Van

Zant. She rubs my sleeve between her fingers. "Really sophisticated."

"And get this," Chloe adds, so loud that probably everybody out on the concourse can hear it, too, "I saw John Moorehouse in Goodman's Monday, buying a tie. It's the exact same color red. Is that not perfect?"

"Totally perfect," says Dina. She uncaps a tube of lipstick and leans into the mirror. "Too bad he'll be with Kathryn Pease."

"Skank," says Laura Lindner, who's been making herself useless bringing in snacks nobody's eating.

"That she is," Dina agrees. She puts her makeup case back into her tote bag. As she lifts the flap, something bright and plastic falls out. It's the barrel of one of those giant water guns they sell at the toy store. Dina pushes the gun back into her bag as she says, "I really thought John had better taste, you know? I mean, who knew he had a thing for choir geeks?"

Not long ago, I probably would have laughed at that. Any bitching about Kathryn, and I would have been all over it. But now, every word is like a little knife. Who let Laura down here, anyway? And how long have I known Dina? Long enough for her to know I'm a choir geek, too.

"Kathryn's a soggy little nobody," Chloe says. For some reason, that gets everybody giggling. "I wouldn't worry about John, Brooke," she tells me. "We'll get the

King and Queen together yet."

Until now nobody's mentioned my dateless status, and I'd hoped it would stay that way. I didn't want to come to Homecoming in the first place. Coming without a date just makes it worse. Outside of this room it is freezing, but I feel sweaty hot. The space heaters are on too high. My dress is too tight. Chloe's voice is too loud. I have to get out.

I have to talk to Kathryn.

I don't realize I'm going to do it until I'm walking through the concourse and I see her ponytail through the crowd. She's going toward the exit. I start to follow her. Past the ticket booths. Out of the stadium. Down into the parking lot. People notice me as I go by. They start to whisper because I'm in my gown and they're in jeans and coats, waiting for the game to end so they can go home to change for the dance.

The farther away we get, the fewer people there are. Now we're in the parking lot, and it's just the two of us. My heels make a clicking sound on the pavement. Maybe she'll hear me and look back. I hope she does. I hope she doesn't, too, because I have no idea what I'm going to say. Maybe I'll say hi, and she'll say hi, and it'll be like this was all just some big misunderstanding. Like all she's been waiting for is me to break the ice so we can say we're sorry and move on. Maybe I won't have to say

265

I'm sorry. Maybe we can act like the whole thing never happened. Maybe—and this is the weirdest idea of all—maybe I'll ask her to go to New York with me. Or maybe I won't. But I need to talk to her. And now that I'm close to doing it, I feel calmer than I have been in a long time.

Kathryn opens the big double doors that lead into the school. We walk through the art wing, which is dark except for the glow from the fire alarms. We go out into the commons, where blasts of music are coming from the DJ in the gym. We get all the way to Kathryn's locker. And then she stops.

I almost reach out to touch her on the shoulder.

"Um . . . Kathryn?"

She freezes. Slowly, she turns around.

"Brooke." She says it like she's been expecting me. But now that I'm standing in front of her I go blank.

"What do you want?" she says.

"I . . ." What *do* I want, exactly? "I, um . . . thought maybe we could talk."

"Talk . . ." She looks like she doesn't believe me.

"Yeah."

"Okay, let's talk." She steps away from her locker, bringing her face close to mine. "You want me to go home and leave John Moorehouse for you, right? Because God forbid somebody get in the way of something you want."

"No." I try again. "I've been thinking. About the Blackmore . . ."

"Oh right. I'm supposed to bow out there, too. Let you have the spotlight like everybody else does. Is that it?"

"No!"

"Then *what do you want*, Brooke?" She leans in closer. "Seriously. What do you want from me?"

"I don't know!" I say, totally confused now. "I've just . . . I've been thinking."

She crosses her arms. Lifts her chin. And she manages to look down her nose at me even though she's a good foot shorter. "About what? New ways to humiliate me? Was punching me in the face not enough?"

Okay. It's fair for her to bring that up. In all the time since it happened I never said I was sorry.

"God, that," I say. "That was . . ." I start to say "a mistake," but she interrupts.

"I should have known you'd never let me live that down. After all this time you're still punishing me. I can't wait to see what you come up with tonight."

Now I'm totally confused. Why do I get the feeling we're not just talking about a few dirty looks in choir here?

"Punishing you how?" I say. "What are you talking about?"

"Come on, Brooke. Getting people to donate money

for choir dresses? I got that one loud and clear. My mom and dad aren't rich like yours are. I guess that's hilarious, right?"

I'm speechless. Honestly, I wasn't thinking about Kathryn at all with the choir dress thing. I was trying to do something nice. And if I *was* thinking about her, maybe somewhere deep inside that I'm not totally aware of, then it was one thing that didn't come out of my angry side. I really did want to help.

"But that's not enough," she goes on. "It's never enough with you. No, I get this." She reaches into her locker and pulls out a plastic package. She shoves it into my hands. I look down and read the label—INFANT WATER WINGS: FOR PRESWIMMERS. When I look up, she's pulling out more stuff. There are snorkels. Creepy Photoshopped pictures. A pamphlet about CPR. Way too much for me to hold. They start to fall out of my arms, onto the floor.

That doesn't stop Kathryn. She keeps pulling things out, throwing them into a pile at my feet.

"I've had it," she says. "I don't deserve to be tormented because you can't stand the idea that somebody might actually beat you at something for once in your life."

"Hey, wait!" I say. Because this is it—what I wanted to talk about. How, even though we hurt each other in the past, maybe if we can come back to music, then it wouldn't matter who won. Maybe it would be enough just to not feel so alone anymore. "About the Black-more . . ."

But she keeps talking.

"I actually can't wait for the Blackmore, Brooke. Because you can try to ruin my Homecoming, but you can't control how I do when it's just me up there on that stage. And tonight? I am going to stay and dance. I don't care what you do to me, because this time I know I haven't done anything wrong."

"I'm not going to *do* anything," I say. But she isn't listening. She reaches into her purse and takes out a piece of paper. It's Pepto-Bismol pink—the invitation to Chloe's party from last year.

This she holds out.

"Take it," she says. Her eyes are blazing with hatred. "Take all of it."

I stare at the paper. Then down at the water toys at my feet. And I flash back to Laura Lindner under my gazebo, laughing while Kathryn almost drowned. Laura in choir. Laura following Chloe around like a desperate little animal.

Kathryn kicks a SCUBA action figure. It goes skidding across the floor. I bend down to pick everything up. When I'm back on my feet, she looks me right in the eye and stares until it's me who has to turn away. I have to bend over sideways to get the invitation, but I manage to grab it from her hand. Then I hurry back down the hallway, leaving her there by her locker.

I know exactly where I'm going.

"There you are, Brooke!" says Chloe. The Homecoming court is standing on the side of the football field, waiting for halftime to start. On the track sits a line of old convertibles we're supposed to ride in. It's all very Hollywood. Or at least it will be once the ceremony gets going. Right now, everybody is huddled in a group, and Chloe is running around with a half-empty box of boutonnieres. When she sees me, she comes rushing over.

"We've been looking everywhere for you," she tells me. "Where did you go?"

I push past her to find Laura, who is helping match people up with their cars. I jerk her around. Shove the package of water wings at her.

"What is this?" I say.

She looks at the wings like she's surprised to see them. Then she glances at Chloe and laughs.

"It's just a little game we've been playing. I thought you'd like it."

"Laura told us about your choir party," Chloe says. "Come on, Brooke, you have to admit it's pretty funny. And besides, didn't you say you wanted Kathryn out of your way?"

On the field, the players are close to scoring. I can see John a few yards away by the goal post, crouching for the play. Laura has to shout over the cheering crowd.

"I was just trying to help," she says. "I mean Kathryn Pease and John Moorehouse? She totally screwed you over, Brooke."

Wait a minute.

How did Laura find out I liked John? Nobody knew. Nobody except . . .

Oh.

I am *such* an idiot.

I shoot Chloe a look that could freeze fire. Then I pull myself up so that I tower over Laura. "I don't want your help," I snarl. "I don't *need* your help. Stay away from Kathryn, and stay away from me."

"Hey. Brooke." Laura's face has turned gray. "Don't be mad. We were only . . ."

I don't give her a chance to finish. I'm halfway across the field before Chloe plants herself in front of me.

"Brooke, come on. . . ."

Over Chloe's shoulder, the scoreboard is ticking away the last seconds of the quarter.

"Leave Kathryn alone," I tell her. "This is between me and her."

She laughs. "You aren't serious."

"I'm dead serious. Leave her alone."

The Pirates have scored a touchdown. The crowd gets even louder.

"So this is all the thanks I get?" Chloe shouts. "I'm only looking out for you, Brooke."

"You're looking out for yourself."

"Excuse me?" She squares up and stares. "This is just priceless. Kathryn stabs you in the back yet again, and you're worried about her. But do I get any appreciation? No. All I ever do is try to help you, Brooke."

"Did you ever stop to think that I don't want your help?"

"You *need* my help. You're the most popular person at this school, but without me you'd make a total waste of it. Like right now. You're ruining Homecoming over some stupid music freak."

The marching band is behind me now, getting ready to head onto the field. The director yells at us to move out of the way. I stay put.

"I told you I didn't care about Homecoming."

Chloe's nostrils start to flare. Her breath comes out in angry puffs. "Which is probably the most selfish thing I've ever heard," she says. "There are people who would kill to be where you are right now."

"People like you?" I take a step forward, trying to scare her like I did Laura. "If I have a problem with Kathryn, it's between her and me. Nobody else."

But Chloe shakes her head.

"Maybe you should have thought about that before you hit her in front of fifty other people. Maybe you should have considered it before you spent the past year using the atomic Dempsey power to make her a complete and total outcast. The whole school knows you hate Kathryn Pease, and if you hate somebody, they're going to hate her, too. She's fair game as far as we're concerned."

The scoreboard buzzer goes off and the marching band starts walking around us. I duck to keep from getting hit in the head with a trombone slide.

"If I started it, then I'm ending it," I say. "What if I told you I thought she was great? That we were best friends? You'd be slobbering all over her again, just like last year."

"Nope, sorry." Chloe smiles an evil smile and shrugs like the whole thing is out of her hands. "Sorority rush is over, Brooke. Kathryn is a nobody. I gave her a chance to stay away tonight, and she ignored me. Whatever happens now, she asked for it."

KATHRYN

WHAT DID I COME HERE for? My locker stands open, waiting for me to take from it what I came to take, only I can't remember what that was. The hallway is eerily quiet now that Brooke's voice and my voice no longer echo through it. I stand, gripping the locker door as my gaze darts from the coat hook to the books stacked on the top shelf, to the Met Opera mug that holds my pencils and pens.

Oh right. A pen.

I take one from the mug, and as I do the edges of the world start to shimmer—is it tears or adrenaline, or is everything changing now that we've broken the silence that has grown between us for so long?

I close my locker and slide to the floor with my back against the door, letting my heart rate slow, screwing my eyes shut so that when I open them the world will be solid again. I can't go back to Elise and the *Picayune* table; I can't go back to interviewing people about their Homecoming memories. Whatever was going to happen tonight, it's started.

I stand and make my way back through school, back into the night. As I walk through the parking lot I think about Matt at home in front of his computer, typing conversations with online friends who are more real to him than real life these days. Without Matt, I am untethered—floating free without anything to anchor me.

A sharp buzz sounds; it's the scoreboard, announcing the end of the first half. From inside the stadium I can hear the crowd cheering, hear the school fight song, hear the announcer boom out the halftime score. I pick up my pace, hurrying because if John is going to wear the crown and the cape, then I at least owe it to him to be there to see it.

Emerging from the concourse and into the bleachers, I see football players running toward the field house. The stadium lights dim and search lights come on, arcing through the sky like enormous magic wands. The marching band begins to file onto the field as a new voice comes over the PA system: "Welcome, students, parents, teachers, and alumni to the William O. Douglas High School seventy-fifth annual Homecoming celebration!"

Convertibles are lined up along the sidelines, each carrying a member of the Homecoming court. I can see

Brooke in the second car, elegant in a black-and-red dress, and John in the fifth, still wearing his football uniform.

The convertibles make their way toward a stage that has been set up in the middle of the field with a platform on top, where the King and Queen will get their crowns. The convertibles drop off the candidates, who line up on the lower level with Chloe orchestrating the spectacle as only Chloe can.

Here in the stands, people seem to know the winners before Ms. Van Whye can announce them. "Moorehouse, Moorehouse!" they start to chant. Tim McNamara sneaks behind me and picks up my arms, making me clap like a big, overgrown seal. "What's wrong?" he says when I jump away. "Don't you want to stand by your man?"

"He's not . . ." I begin, only to be drowned out by cheers as John's name is, in fact, called. I shake Tim off so that I can clap on my own, while John shuffles up to the platform and Ms. Van Whye places an oversized crown on his head.

They're chanting for Brooke now, and Tim approaches as if he's going to make me clap again. I step away, with a glare that stops him cold.

"Brooke! Brooke! Brooke!" everybody shouts.

And they're right about that, too, as if there was ever any doubt.

Brooke steps forward, Chloe by her side, like a monarch with her lady-in-waiting. Chloe straightens Brooke's sweater, making sure she is ready to receive her crown, then they start up the stairs to the platform.

Brooke has always been the Queen B; only this time, it's official.

BROOKE

IT'S FREEZING ON THE STAGE. Way colder than it was on the field. But Chloe had a hissy fit about people wearing coats over their gowns, so we left them under the concourse with the rest of our stuff.

Hold on. . . .

The water gun in Dina's bag.

The giggles when Chloe talked about getting me and John together.

The junk in Kathryn's locker.

Whatever happens tonight, she asked for it.

Oh my God.

Chloe stands next to me, applauding as Ms. Van Whye pins a red cape to John's shoulder pads. "Chloe," I say. "What are you going to do?" She doesn't answer. I reach behind and pinch the back of her arm. "Chloe! At the dance. What are you going to do to Kathryn?"

Chloe squeals, but not because of me. In fact, I barely

got any flesh in my fingers because Ms. Van Whye just announced Queen and Chloe's hands flew up to her mouth, like a beauty pageant winner.

"Oh my God!" she screams. "Did you hear that, Brooke? They just called your name!"

She bolts for the podium. When I don't automatically follow she turns back, clapping her hands together. "This is it. Aren't you excited? We won!" Then she starts up the steps like it's her who's getting the crown. I step forward and yank her back.

"I mean it, Chloe. Leave Kathryn alone."

The other people onstage are laughing. To them it looks like we've gotten tangled up—like Chloe's tripped or I've goosed her, just for fun. Chloe balances herself. Then she reaches out to straighten my sweater. "Don't worry about Kathryn," she says. "Everybody will have fun tonight, I promise. Even her, if she takes it the right way."

She tries for the steps again, but I hang on and say the one thing that has any chance of getting through.

"If you touch Kathryn . . . If *anybody* does *anything* tonight, I swear to God I will do to you what I did to her."

Chloe stares at me with that Miss America grin. She either doesn't believe me or she doesn't understand.

"I'm serious," I tell her. "Touch Kathryn, and I will spend the entire rest of this year making you a leper."

"Like you would." Chloe tries to shake free. "After everything I've done for you?"

I bring back all of the blackness—the horrible, awful, awesomely powerful feeling that came with punching Kathryn—and I swing right for where I know it will hurt.

"Think about it," I tell Chloe. "You've got the whole rest of this semester and the whole semester after that. Plus the summer. That's a long time to be alone. No parties. No friends. No nothing. And Bill and Brice have contacts all over the place. College might not be that much better."

The other candidates are motioning us to keep moving. Up in the stands, people have started stomping their feet. They're waiting for the halftime show to be over. They don't know that the real show is right here, between Chloe and me.

Doubt starts to creep across her face. But Chloe didn't get where she is by giving up easily.

"I don't need you," she tells me.

"Then try it," I shoot back. "Remember what I did to her? Remember how bad it got? I can do it to you, too. Easy."

"Girls?" Ms. Van Whye gestures for us to get up there and get on with it.

"It's a power thing," I say. "That's what you always told me. People keep track of who's on my bad side so they don't end up there, too."

Chloe's smile starts to lose its edge. I can see her weighing up everything I've said. Calculating her odds. She opens her mouth. Then she shuts it again. She tosses her razored hair, but she doesn't look anywhere near as confident as before.

And then, she looks away.

"If anyone does anything," I repeat, "I don't care who, it's all coming back on you. So if I were you, I'd spread the word fast."

I go past her, up onto the podium. Ms. Van Whye hands me a bouquet of roses. John kisses my hand. And Chloe makes her way over with a tiara.

"You don't deserve any of this," she tells me as she reaches up to put the crown in my hair.

I reach up, too, like I'm going to help. What I really do is dig my fingernails into her wrist. She gasps, and I give a little shake. Just so she knows I haven't forgotten my promise.

"When have I ever deserved it?" I say.

KATHRYN

"SHALL I GET THE DOOR for you, your highness?"

Bud Dawes races ahead of us, up to the big double doors that lead inside the school. John sighs, draping his cape over one arm and cradling his crown in the other. "Call me 'your highness' again, 'Dawg, and I'll kick your ass."

I take long, deep breaths as we near the entrance; my back tingles, expecting Bud to slam the door on me. "Nice dress," he says. Is he being sarcastic? I can't tell, but I say "thank you" anyway in a voice that surprises me with its steadiness before it echoes away through the empty commons.

Though it is quiet out here, the gym is brimming over with people. I hold my head up as we enter, taking rapid inventory: Starfish dangle from the ceiling, blue lights waver on the floor, fishing nets hang from the walls, and a woman in a mermaid costume serves punch. It's an underwater theme.

Of course it is.

Well-wishers swarm around John: guys clamoring to high-five him and girls waiting their turn to give him a hug. The guys smile, not unkindly, at me, but the girls keep their distance, which isn't much different from the way things usually are, except that now I see aggression in the tiniest of gestures:

Kiersten Coons is whispering something to Violet Alexander, no doubt debating whether to dump mud or motor oil down the front of my dress.

Angela Van Zant keeps glancing in my direction, probably making sure I'm standing in just the right spot.

Dina scratches her nose: Is that the signal?

John rests a hand on my shoulder. "You okay?"

I jump. "Why? Should I not be?"

"Whoa." He lifts both hands as if he's just touched something hot. "Looks like I hit a nerve."

What am I supposed to say? I know I'm making an ass out of myself, but the truth is that I don't trust him; I don't trust anybody. The dark gym with its gyrating bodies, loud music, and seashell-laced ceiling could be one huge booby trap.

"I'm going to the restroom," I tell him before scurrying off to the one place I know will at least have decent lighting.

This is wrong, I think as I sit in a stall, listening to people coming and going. *I should have let Brooke have John. I should have come with Matt like we'd planned all along.* If I had come with him, then I wouldn't even be here right now; we would have taken one look at the DJ booth with its papier mâché shipwreck decorations, giggled, and then went back to my house, where a collector's edition of *Buffy the Vampire Slayer* waits on my DVD player. Instead I am a walking target. I come close to pulling up my feet and crouching on the toilet for the rest of the evening, but Brooke's face has been burned into my brain. If I disappear I might be safe, but I will have given her exactly what she wants.

No. Brooke, Chloe, Dina—even John if he somehow turns out to be in on the plot: I won't give them the satisfaction of seeing me broken again. No matter what they do, I won't shatter.

I'm not made of glass.

I stand, smooth the wrinkles from my dress, and venture out of the stall to find Laura Lindner at the sink, washing her hands. She glares at my reflection in the mirror, the first person to make eye contact all evening. Perhaps because I need to test my voice or perhaps because I actually care, I say, "I've been where you are, you know."

"Been where?" she says, eyeing me with disdain.

"With Chloe and those guys. I know how good it feels when they like you. I also know how hard it is to fit in. As soon as you make a mistake or you aren't useful to them anymore, they'll drop you."

"What are you, jealous or something?" she sneers.

"Not really," I say, which, I realize, is true. I remember how good it felt to be with Chloe, Dina, and the others, but I also see now just how perilous it was. If nothing else, tonight is a chance to brush myself off and walk away—something I didn't get to do that night so many months ago.

I leave Laura in the bathroom and head back to the gym to find the Homecoming court gathered at the DJ booth. Everyone cheers as Ms. Van Whye presents Brooke and John in full royal regalia. Bud Dawes prances out wearing an Honors Choir gown, and the entire room breaks into laughter. He hands Brooke a big cardboard check; next year a new singer will get her choir dress for free with enough money left over to help three others, too, since Brooke has raised a record amount. I find myself smiling at the idea of somebody we don't know— maybe a freshman ten times more talented than Brooke or I will ever be—getting something good out of such a bitter rivalry.

The lights dim and a spotlight illuminates a circle of empty floor; it's time for the King and Queen to dance

with each other. John reaches for Brooke, but she shakes her head, turning instead to Bud, who bows and kisses her hand. When he tries to lead her out to dance, however, she sends him into the arms of one of the other King candidates, sparking another round of catcalls.

John peers into the crowd, searching for, then spotting me. *Come here*, he mouths.

I shake my head. No matter how brave I might have felt five minutes ago, right now I am positively petrified.

Come here, John mouths again.

I take a step, every nerve ending abuzz. Nothing happens. I take two more, then another two, whispers following me the entire way, until I reach the place where John stands. Music starts and I stiffen in his arms. I can't take my eyes off of Brooke; whatever she has planned, I want to see it coming.

"I'm starting to think I've got cooties," John says as we begin to sway. "Is hanging out with me really that horrible?"

"No," I tell him. "It's . . ." As soon as I start to speak, Brooke steps off the stage and strides with purpose toward John and me. I steel myself for the blow, for the drenching spray, for the paint balls to start raining down, but Brooke keeps walking, moving past us to the exit.

She's leaving?

No; she stops. Through glimmering blue lights I see her hold out both hands to someone: a boy in jeans and an *Empire Strikes Back* sweatshirt.

"What the . . . ," says John. "Isn't that your friend?"

It is. It's Matt, letting Brooke lead him through the sea of gowns and suits to the spotlit circle where John and I stand. Neither of them will look at me, even though we are just a few feet away from one another. I crane my neck, searching for Chloe, Dina, the rest of them. I find Chloe in the DJ booth, looking down on us with an expression blank as stone.

This is worse than having my dress ruined, worse than being ignored, even worse than being punched in the face.

And worst of all is knowing I deserve it.

"I wouldn't have pegged Brooke for a guy like that," John says. Matt and Brooke are dancing now, so close to us that we nearly brush up against one another. "But I guess you never know, now, do you?"

"No," I say. We move miserably from side to side—or at least *I* am miserable; John is just quiet. Around us, the chatter about Brooke and Matt starts to die down. People have had enough of the novelty; they're getting impatient to dance.

"Can I ask you something?" I say to John.

"Sure," he replies.

"Why did you ask me here tonight?"

He turns a little as we sway, and soon I am looking at the other end of the gym, which is a relief because I can no longer see Matt with his back to me and Brooke with her cheek on his shoulder.

"Who else would I ask?" he says.

I smile bitterly; if he's joking, it's a good act. But I have to know: Is he in on the plot or isn't he?

"Well, it's not as if we really know each other. You hang out with one group of people, I hang out with . . ." The only name to put in that space would be Matt's, so I let the sentence trail off, leaving a void that mirrors the one inside of me.

John shrugs. "I had fun working with you in Anatomy, and you keep to yourself so much I thought maybe you'd like to get out. Plus, I knew you'd look great tonight, and you do. Is that a shallow reason?"

"No," I say. The rose-colored gown *is* beautiful; after all the pain I've caused, I'm glad someone is able to appreciate it.

"I guess the easy answer," John says, "is that I asked you because I wanted to."

I should leave it there; I should shut my mouth and just enjoy being in the arms of someone who's kind and understanding and genuinely wants to be here with me, but I just can't do it. "Chloe must have told you about me," I press. "Didn't she tell you about what happened last year?"

"I heard a few things, but I didn't necessarily believe them." John pushes me backward so he can peer into my eyes. "I wasn't here last fall, so whatever happened back then means zilch to me. Why do you care what Chloe and those guys think, anyway?"

And that is the question, the one that has been dogging me: *Why?* I've been so obsessed over what happened with Brooke—so consumed by thoughts of getting even or getting something back or whatever it is I've been seeking, that I failed to appreciate the real friendship I had with Matt.

Or with Brooke, back when it was just the two of us.

The dance is nearing its end. There are no falling fishnets, no water balloons, no ambushes or flying snorkel gear; just Matt twirling Brooke, making her laugh like she used to when we would stay up late on the phone or hog the karaoke machine at the coffee shop, making fun of the singers on *American Idol*.

The music fades, the spotlight blinks off, and the space where we have been slow-dancing fills with bodies moving to a fast song I barely know. John moves with them while I bob halfheartedly along. Matt and Brooke have been swallowed up in the crowd; I can't see them anymore.

"You're not having fun, are you?" says John.

I try to smile, but I know it looks weak.

"I'm sorry," I say. "You've been wonderful tonight. Really. I'm just not feeling well, and I don't think I'd be any fun if I stayed. You don't have to leave, though. Stay here with your friends."

"But your car's back at my house."

"Oh. God." I bury my head in my hands. Since John lives closer to school than I do, we went to his place to change after the game, and my car is still sitting on the street in front of his house.

"It's okay," he says. "I'll give you a ride."

"Or I could do it."

Matt's voice comes from just over my shoulder. I turn to see him beside me. The nerves that have been fraying all night finally snap; the anger—at myself, at Brooke, at Matt—and the humiliation of seeing him with her boil over. Before I can think about what I'm doing, I wrench away from John and bolt for the door.

"Kath!" Matt shouts after me. "Kath!"

He catches up with me in the parking lot, grabs my elbow, brings me around, and kisses me. It's a surprisingly gentle kiss, all things considered. I suppose I've been anticipating it ever since that first day in Sunday school so many years ago.

But it's wrong. I can't describe why, exactly—it just

isn't *us*. Not that I wouldn't have been willing to change us, if it felt right; I've thought about this, in those rare moments when I allowed myself to wonder what being more than friends would actually be like. But now that I've experienced it, I know.

Is Matt your boyfriend? If I ever had a doubt, I know now that the answer is no. We know each other too well.

Which is why *he* should have known what coming to Homecoming with Brooke would do to me.

"What were you doing in there?" I demand. *"What were you doing?!"*

"I was dancing," he says.

I smack his chest with my open palm. "You know what I mean. Why are you here with her? *Her* of all people?"

Matt still holds my elbow, and as he moves in to kiss me again I pull back. This time I'm better able to process what I'm feeling, even if I can't quite put it into words.

"I don't . . . ," I stammer, "I mean, I can't . . ."

Disappointment, resignation, and even a bit of relief play across his features. He pulls back and lets me go.

"I know," he says.

He looks so sweet, so sensible, so *Matt* that my anger starts to fade. It's so good having him here—having him back—that I almost forget why we were fighting. To remind myself, I picture him dancing with Brooke again.

"And besides," I say, "what are you doing even talking to me after what you just did? Was that the plan? She's using *you* to hurt me now?"

But he just smiles that *come on* smile, with those eyes that have seen through me since we were eight years old.

"After everything you've pulled, you're giving me hell for this? You've done some stupid things, Kath, but you're not dumb. Brooke called because she thought you might need me and you know what? It kind of looks like you do."

He unknots his coat from around his waist and holds it up. My teeth are chattering, still I hesitate one stubborn second more, hanging on to the last shred of an anger I know I've got no right to.

"But not like this," I tell him. I gesture toward the gym door. "That back there—it was terrible!"

"Okay." He tosses his coat over his shoulder and turns to walk away. "That dress is way too beautiful to cover up anyway."

Shame washes from the top of my head all the way down to my toes, and I promise myself that, as soon as I get home, I am going to put the rose-colored gown into the back of my closet; I will wear my Honors Choir gown for the Blackmore—it will have to do.

I scurry to catch up with him. He stands with his

arms out until, finally, I step into the warmth of his jacket.

"It's still early," he says. "I've got the super-duper, extraspecial extended edition director's cut *Two Towers* DVD back at my place. Wanna watch it?"

Laughing, I nod as he helps me into his car and then puts the key in the ignition.

"That's what I've been missing," he says. "The Matt Melter. Seems I can't go too long without it."

"You forgot the tee em," I pout.

"No I didn't. I just wanted to hear you say it."

He pulls out of the school parking lot and starts driving toward my house. We ride silently for blocks, but it's a comfortable silence, and when we pass a bank of fast food restaurants he pulls into a drive-through. He orders the greasiest items on the menu for us to eat during our movie. Then, as we wait for the pickup window, he says, "So. John Moorehouse, huh?"

I moan, my cheeks going hot. "If I ever had a chance with him I'm sure I ruined it. He probably thinks I was the worst date ever."

"At least you had a date."

I look over at him and he looks back at me. I have so much to apologize for that I barely know where to start. "I know," I say. "What I did really sucked. I should have come with you like I'd promised. I'm sorry."

He pulls the car forward, takes out his wallet, and hands the girl at the window his money.

"I wasn't talking about me," he says. "I was talking about Brooke."

BROOKE

KATHRYN JUST LEFT. THERE'S NOTHING more for me to do here.

In the locker room, crammed in with my regular swimming gear, are eight Super Soaker guns, a water balloon launcher, and five packages of balloons that never got filled. Out in my car there's a huge fishing net and a bag of lifeguard's whistles. After halftime, I made Dina and Laura empty out their bags. Chloe got the message to anyone else who wasn't in the Homecoming court.

And on my way to the dance I called Matt.

Standing by the DJ booth, I look out at the gym. John is buddying around with the football players. Chloe is giving fashion advice to some new sophomore she's decided to adopt. Laura Lindner is hanging around the edges, trying to look like she belongs. In two weeks I'll be onstage at the Blackmore. All that's left after that is spring semester; then I'll be out of here and I'll probably never see these people again.

The DJ plays an old Billy Idol song. People start chanting along, which makes my throat hurt just listening to it. Dr. Dunne told me I didn't have nodes, but he did see polyps starting to form. He gave me a bunch of exercises to do, plus a lecture on taking better care of my voice. No way I'm going to try to yell over all this noise.

I'm getting out of here.

I go around the crowd, weaving through the teachers so nobody on the dance floor will see me. The ticket table is deserted. As I walk past, I take the crown out of my hair and toss it onto the table. Chloe can have it if it means that much to her.

I don't look back as I walk out of the gym. Now that I've done my job, I can finally leave.

SENIOR YEAR

*Resolution: the changing of a dissonant pitch to create a
group of tones that are harmonious to the ear*

KATHRYN

THE BANNERS WENT UP OVER the week-
end—big red swaths of silk cascading from the entries of
every building on the Baldwin campus, each one embla-
zoned with a golden B for Blackmore. Monday I took the
long way to school so I could see the streamers on the
Main Street light posts: crimson and cheerful against
the November sky. The local paper is filled with breath-
less stories about the new recital hall, as if nobody can
believe that the festival is really going to happen like
the organizers promised it would, albeit a month and
several days late. And yesterday on my way to my voice
lesson, I caught a glimpse of Margaret Frist-Stallworth,
the Met's new contralto, going into the opera workshop
theater. If competitors weren't banned from talking to
judges I would have asked her for an autograph.

The banners, the streamers, the famous people
arriving in our tiny town—they're a reminder of what

waits for me at the end of these last, grueling two weeks. The day after Homecoming, I spent the morning with Mr. Lieb and my accompanist, the afternoon with the Honors Choir, and the evening writing my post-Homecoming feature for the *Picayune*. I started my AP English paper around midnight, but fell asleep waiting for our dial-up to download the formatting requirements from Ms. Amos's website.

Monday when I tried to explain, she sat me down and offered up a story.

"When I was in college I wanted to be an actress," she told me. "Junior year, I got the lead in the annual production, *The Taming of the Shrew*, and I spent every waking minute in rehearsals. When my American Lit professor informed me I was failing his class I told him how busy I was, thinking surely he'd cut me some slack. His response is something I remember to this day. He said we all have choices to make, and we make those choices based on what is really important to us. If passing American Literature was important to me, then I would find a way to pass it. If not, then I would have to accept the consequences, though he hoped I would do so without regret. I flunked that quarter, but do you know what? It was the best three months of my life."

I looked at her, blankly.

"Thanks," I said.

"It's no trouble," she replied. "I'll know your choice when I see your next assignment."

So what was my choice? I did it all. I passed the Anatomy test, I stayed up all of Monday night writing an A-plus English paper, and Saturday at regionals I sang flawlessly, helping the Honors Choir earn the top score, which will send us on to State in the spring.

And now, the Blackmore is just one day away.

I'm lying under the covers in my room, hitting snooze on my alarm clock, when my mother peeks through the door.

"You're not up yet," she says. "Aren't you going to go to school?"

"I don't feel well," I tell her. "I think I'm going to stay home."

I move over so she can sit on the side of my bed, letting her feel my forehead for fever. "Is everything okay?" she asks.

"Yes." I rest my cheek against her cool hand. "I just . . . need the rest."

"I understand. You've got a big day tomorrow."

I close my eyes. Her words have melted the hardness I've been trying to build up inside of myself, and the tears threaten to spill over; it's the first time she's mentioned the Blackmore directly to me.

"I have something for you," she continues. "I was

going to bring it out after school but since you're not going, maybe you'd like to take a look now."

She disappears into her bedroom and returns minutes later with an armful of midnight blue. She drops one arm, and I gasp as out unfurls a ball gown with capped sleeves, a fairy-tale skirt, and a dusting of glitter on the bodice.

"I'm sorry this went until the last minute, but I wanted to surprise you and you're up until all hours of the night these days. I had to steal whatever time I could get while you were at your voice lessons."

I climb out of bed and walk around to finger the voluminous layers of the skirt. "It's beautiful, Mom," I murmur. "Really gorgeous."

"I knew you needed a dress for the competition," she says, then frowns at the sight of me in my T-shirt and underwear. "Though you've lost so much weight, I may have to take it in. Stay here while I go get my sewing kit."

I'm standing on a stack of books, Mom circling me with pins in her mouth, when Dad comes in carrying a bagel in one hand, morning coffee in the other.

"Well if you aren't the prettiest girl there ever was," he says. "Maybe you should drop music and take up modeling instead."

He watches, sipping his coffee, while Mom cinches the gown so that it fits like a second skin. When she unzips me to adjust the bra inside of the bodice, he looks away, out the window at the bullet-colored sky.

"It's supposed to snow," he muses. "Could be bad news for the Blackmore folks if the roads get too icy."

"They can't postpone the contest again," I tell him. "The whole town will flip out."

"Well, then maybe there'll be less competition for you."

I hesitate, then decide that since we all of a sudden are talking about it, I'm going to get everything out in the open.

"Do you think I need less competition? You've barely said anything about the Blackmore these past few months. Do you think I'm not good enough?"

"Oh, honey." Mom rushes around so she can take my face in her hands. "No, no! That's not it at all. It's just that you have so much pressure on you, and we didn't want to make it worse. We know how hard you've been working—sometimes I think too hard."

"But a lot is riding on this," I say, sounding more desperate than I want to. "It's a lot of money. I mean, think what we could do with it."

Dad laughs. "Like a trip around the world?"

"Or my college tuition."

He stops laughing. "We'll find the money for that. You don't have to worry about it."

"Yes, but think how much easier it would be if I won."

Now he's the one standing in front of me, taking my hands in his.

"Sweetpea." He hasn't called me that in a long time; I've missed it. "You've been to the Blackmore. You know how big it is. There are dozens of other people competing; how can you put all of that pressure on yourself?"

"Somebody from here has won it for the past two years," I tell him.

"They've been incredibly lucky. And the odds are even tougher now because of that. I'm not trying to be negative, honey, but your mother and I, we need to know you won't be devastated if things don't work out like you're hoping."

"I know the odds," I tell him. "Brooke Dempsey will win it if I don't."

"Brooke Dempsey," says Mom, placing one last pin and then standing back to admire her handiwork. "Isn't that your friend from last year?"

"Yes."

"Whatever happened to her?"

"She . . . ," I begin, but then stop. To tell them everything would take forever, and I am only just now starting to understand it myself.

"Nothing happened," I say. "We just didn't end up being as close as we'd thought we were."

BROOKE

IT'S TOO LATE TO GO to New York. Hildy picked out the rest of my Blackmore music and we polished it with no help from my dad. I keep calling him, though. More than anything now, it's like I'm on a mission to just get somebody on the phone.

Wednesday, I finally do it. I'm listening to the ring, expecting voice mail to pick up like always. Suddenly there's a click and, "Hello?"

"Jake!" I can't believe I'm actually hearing a real person. "Jake, it's Brooke! Where's my dad?"

"Oklahoma. I thought you were my business manager. She's supposed to be calling any minute."

I push ahead. Screw Jake's business manager. "I tried Dad's cell. I've been trying for weeks but he never answers it."

"That's because he has no time. Did he tell you how insane this new production is? The director fancies himself so avant-garde he can't possibly communicate his vision without driving everybody else mad. Whenever *I* reach your father—which is not often, believe me—he sounds absolutely shattered."

I stand up. Start pacing, and I hear my voice get louder, but I don't bother hiding how pissed I am, because if anybody should be reaching my dad, it's me. "He knows I've got this competition," I say. "He knows what a big deal this is."

"Brooke," Jake interrupts. "Relax."

"Excuse me?"

"I said relax. It's just music."

Did I hear him right?

Tell me he didn't just say that.

"It's not 'just music' to me," I shout. "I'm building a career here, Jake. I thought you of all people would get that."

"I get it," he says. "Loud and clear."

"So why are you giving me this 'relax' crap?"

"Darling." He says it like he's talking to a three-year-old. "Take it from someone who knows. You've got a lot of big auditions ahead of you. If you get wound this tight about every one, you're going to be burnt out by the time you hit thirty. This is a tough business. If you're serious about singing for a living, then you'd better know why you are, and it damned well better be because you love it."

I have to bite my tongue to keep from screaming. Who the hell is Jake Jaspers to be telling me this? I sing because I have to. Because ever since Dad put me up in front of an audience, I have thought about nothing but getting that feeling back again.

"Look, Jake. You don't know what it's like to be living in the ass crack of Minnesota. You don't know about the Blackmore, and you don't know anything about me or what I love or what I can handle, okay?" I have a lump in my throat the size of a grapefruit. I swallow it down. I will *not* cry in front of him. I won't. "This is all I've ever wanted to do."

"Then leave it for a while," he says. "Go to the movies. Take a bubble bath."

He sounds distracted. Like he's about to hang up on me. I can't let him go. I haven't even asked the most important thing yet.

"But what about my dad? He's coming, right? It's okay if he shows up at the last minute. He does that all the time. I just want to make sure he's going to be there."

Jake doesn't say anything for a second. In the background, I hear paper rustling.

"When is this contest again?" he says.

The skin on my shoulders starts to prickle like it always does when something's been forgotten.

"Tomorrow. I've been leaving emails and messages

about it for three months. He knows when it is. He's got to have his plane tickets and everything by now, right?"

More not saying anything.

"Right, Jake?"

"Well . . ." He rustles the papers some more. "It's not written down in the schedule. But don't panic. It could be he just forgot to tell me about the trip."

"Well can you double-check? Can you call him?"

"I'll try." Now his voice sounds less full of itself. "It's just that I don't know when I'll be able to reach him. He's so busy with this damned opera. I don't want you to let this affect your performance, though. If Bill knew this was important, I'm sure he's taken care of it."

But I know he probably hasn't. He probably hasn't even listened to all of my messages to know when the Blackmore is. And even if he is planning on showing up at the last minute, what makes him think that's okay? He obviously didn't think about what this would do to me, or he would have called by now.

I tell Jake thank you. Hang up the phone. Then— finally—I let out the tears.

I take the picture of Dad and me off the top of my piano, the one of us at that stupid party where he dressed me up like a milkmaid and made me sing "The Sound of Music" for all of his friends. I want to throw the picture across the room, but that would be cheesy. I feel stupid for even thinking about it. So I put the picture back, facedown.

I need to do *something*, though.

The old book of Sondheim songs is sitting on the piano bench. I pick it up, open it, and put one hand on either side of the spine. I yank my right hand down, tearing the paper with a big, satisfying rip. I kneel down and start to pull out all the pages. Then I rip those into smaller pieces. I'm not crying anymore. I'm focused. When I'm done, I've got a pile of paper shreds on the floor in front of me. If I had some matches I would set it on fire. But this is Mom's house. The house she pays for with virtually no help from Dad, and I don't want to be the one who destroys it.

Looks like I won't be getting any help from him, either.

KATHRYN

"DELIVERY FOR KATHRYN PEASE."

Knuckles rap on my practice room door, followed by a voice that is cruelly calm considering all that's at stake today. I pause in the middle of a scale and put my hand to my chest, as if that will slow my heartbeat. Roseanne, my accompanist, stops playing as Mr. Lieb goes to the door. He thanks the hall monitor and returns with a vase full of white and pink roses.

"To great performances and second chances," he reads from the card attached. "Love, John. Looks like you've got an admirer?"

I feel myself blush as I take the vase and set it on the piano. This is the second good-luck gift John has given me; Thursday in Anatomy he left a bag filled with lemon drops and bottled water on my seat.

"So what's the right way to say good luck for something like this?" he'd asked. "Break a leg? Bust a vocal cord?"

"How about just 'see you there'?" I'd answered. "I've got an extra ticket if you don't mind sitting with Matt and my parents."

"Are you kidding?" he said. "I'd love to!"

I set the roses on top of the piano, next to the bouquet of silk flowers my mom made and the stress troll Matt gave me. Before Mr. Lieb can close the door, another page leans into the room.

"Five minutes, please," she announces. "Five minutes!"

"Now don't panic," Mr. Lieb tells me. "You've got an hour or so before your turn. Let's use it wisely, shall we?"

I nod and fluff out my skirt; then I take a moment to gather my energy into a column that I visualize running from my forehead down through my toes. Roseanne sounds a starting chord, and I begin a slow descending vocalise. As I sing, I try to block out everything but the way the air feels as my diaphragm pushes it past my vocal cords, the way the tone resonates behind my nose and eyes, the spin at the top of my head where the high notes gather before floating out into the space around me. Here in this tiny room it is virtually impossible to hear the voices in the other practice rooms that run up and down the hallway. Dad was right: There are eighty singers in the preliminary round, all of whom sound amazing. Brooke and I are just two among them; what ever made us think we could win?

Another rap: "Group one, please report to the stage."

This is it. Group one is letters A through F. I'm group three—M through R.

"I need to work on 'The Jewel Song,'" I tell Mr. Lieb, suddenly frantic. "The high parts are strained. The coloratura is muddy. . . ."

He just smiles and instructs Roseanne to play an A-flat. "Up the scale, do a turn, then come back down," he says, and gives a quick demonstration.

"But I have so much to fix!"

"If you haven't fixed it by now, you never will."

I'm picking at the seams of my bodice, chewing on my lip. Though I spent most of yesterday in bed, the stress is inviting fatigue right back in again.

"Kathryn." Mr. Lieb's voice is low. Grounded.

"What?"

"You're ready. I have nothing but faith in you."

The calm in his voice loosens the knot in my stomach and I find that I am able to gather myself once again. As minutes stretch into a half hour I let him lead me through exercises that leave my voice supple, my breathing strong, my mind clear and sharp. When we pause, I poke my head into the hallway, flagging down one of the monitors.

"What letter are the singers in the recital hall on now?" I ask.

The monitor murmurs into his walkie-talkie; then he listens as an answer comes crackling back.

"Sounds like the Cs," he says, and I pull my head back inside, where Mr. Lieb and Roseanne are waiting to start a last run-through of my pieces.

"I'm going down for a minute," I tell them. "There's somebody I need to hear."

The new recital hall has a banner hanging over the door: 50 YEARS OF EXCELLENCE—THE BLACKMORE YOUNG ARTISTS' FESTIVAL. When I enter, the lights are dim, all attention directed at the stage, where a baritone sings "Vecchia Zimarra, Senti" from *La Bohème*. As my eyes adjust, I see that the construction crew has put laminate over the unfinished walls; the air smells like fresh paint and sawdust.

I find an empty seat at the back of the hall, listen to the rest of the baritone's performance, and then sit through a soprano and a tenor. They are all outstanding, strong competitors, and I am reminded yet again of just how big this competition really is.

Then Brooke appears on the stage. I hold my breath as she bows to the audience, nodding to her accompanist that she is ready.

I've heard about performers who command the stage, and I used to think it was a meaningless cliché. But no other word can describe the way Brooke looks in her emerald gown as she gazes into the audience with a half smile that would appear arrogant were it not so solid, so confident, so . . . commanding. She begins to sing and I close my eyes. Ages have passed since I've heard her voice by itself, without a chorus of other voices to muddy or mask it, and I imagine I'm listening to someone ten years older, a singer far more advanced than a high school senior has any right to be. Brooke has taken her singing beyond Honors Choir, beyond our rivalry, beyond even the Blackmore, it seems to me. But instead of being intimidated by her, I am calm. Ready. More than anything, I just want to know what it's like to be on that stage, too.

An hour later, I find out.

The lights are incredibly bright when they're shining straight into your eyes, making it so that the audience can see every detail of your performance while all you can make out are faceless silhouettes. For the first several minutes I am hyperaware of every note Roseanne plays, every word I sing. But then, halfway through my second piece, something rare happens: As the music spools from memory out of my throat, I forget about Brooke. I forget about scholarships and my parents and Matt and John, who are sitting together somewhere out in the crowd. This music is beautiful, it is fun to sing, and I am performing it for some of the best musicians in the world.

I'm singing because I can. Not for money, not for recognition, not for revenge.

But simply because it is wonderful.

BROOKE

WE MADE THE FINALS. ME and Kathryn. We're both going on to the end.

For the big announcement, they put everybody in the first two rows of the hall, in reserved seats so the people who don't advance have someplace to watch the rest of the competition. They called my name first. My heart jumped, but I couldn't celebrate. Not until I heard her name, too.

Kathryn got called second to last. She slumped over in relief as her mom and dad reached over her seatback to give her a hug.

Now, we have an hour and a half to go.

The finalists each get their own studios surrounding the greenroom. From the greenroom is a short hallway to backstage. And from there, it's just a few more steps to showtime. Our names were already taped to the doors when they took us back, along with the order we'll be competing in. There are ten of us. I'm number six. Kathryn is eight.

"Brooke, you did it." Hildy rushes in with Joan, my accompanist, and kisses me on both cheeks. She takes two new bottles of water out of her bag. Puts one on the piano and hands the other one to me. "Dr. Dunne's orders," she says. "You need to stay hydrated."

"That felt good," I tell her. "The second round was hard. But I'm good. I feel okay."

"You're more than okay. I wasn't sure you'd be ready, but you pulled it together. Congratulations."

I keep looking past her at the door, expecting it to open and my dad to come in. The whole time I was singing, all through the first two rounds, I pictured him in the audience. He's been a part of this dream from the start, and he always comes through, even if it's at the last minute.

The knob on the door starts to turn. Hildy's voice gets drowned out by the blood rushing in my ears. It's Daddy. He's here.

"Brookie?"

Brice pokes his head in. Bill Jr.'s head pokes in on top of it.

"Hey, there you are," says Bill, looking around. "This is some nice setup you have back here."

"Out of the way, you two." Mom pushes past them

and comes all the way into the room. She holds out her arms to me. "Brooke, you were amazing. I'm so proud of you."

I let her hug me. Over her shoulder I can see into the greenroom. I can see singers hanging out. Other parents. Teachers. But no Dad.

"He didn't come."

"Oh, honey." Mom keeps her arms around me. "I'm sorry. . . ."

I pull away. "Did he call the house? Maybe his plane got delayed because of the snow."

But the look on her face has all the answers I need. Dad isn't here because he didn't try. Didn't care enough. Didn't want to miss his precious work or another vacation with Jake. Whatever. The reasons don't matter. There probably isn't a reason. He'll apologize tomorrow or the next day or whenever he finally realizes what he's done. Then he'll offer to fly me to New York and I'll probably go because even though he let me down I still want to see him.

I still want to be in his world.

"Okay," I say. I start moving around. Taking the lid off my water bottle. Organizing my music. Hildy and Joan hang out in the back, trying not to eavesdrop.

"Honey," says Mom.

"No, really." I gulp some air to push down the lump in

my throat. "It's okay. He's busy."

"No, it isn't okay. I hate that he did this. Today of all days. We all know how much this means to you."

And even though my eyes are burning, it's Mom who starts to cry. This time it's me putting my arms around her. "I'm sorry," she keeps saying. And all I can say is "It's okay."

Because what else is there?

Mercifully, Brice pokes in again. He reaches over Mom's head to hand me a bronze plastic helmet with horns coming out the sides.

"Hey, Brookhilde. You kicked some ass out there."

"We thought about springing for the breastplate, too," says Bill. "And the spear. So you'd have the whole *ensemble*."

I brace for the Amazon joke. I know it's coming.

"But you're way too pretty for that."

"Yeah," adds Brice as he admires my gown. "I'm a little weirded out by the gorgeous, actually. I mean, you've always been Baby B. And now, lately, you're . . . wow!"

I have no choice but to put on the helmet and smack both of them around a little bit. Because otherwise I'll be crying, too, and I'm done with that.

Besides, how gorgeous will I be if I've got mascara running down my cheeks?

In my music bag I've got a thermos of chicken broth,

some apple slices, and a turkey sandwich that I packed this morning. No mayo or cheese. I may not even eat the bread, since the last thing I need is a bunch of phlegm on my vocal cords. Mom and the twins, on the other hand, are starving. So they head out for dinner while I stay back with Hildy and Joan. We do exercises to keep my voice warm. We go over parts of my songs. We practice deep breathing, which is supposed to make me even more focused. And after a while, the countdown starts. Thirty minutes until curtain. Fifteen minutes. Five. I could hang out here until it's time for me to sing. Someone will come get me. But I'm starting to feel *too* focused.

I want to hear what I'm up against.

"I'm going out there," I tell Hildy.

She frowns. "You won't get distracted?"

"No," I tell her. "I'm going."

Out in the greenroom I can hear the other singers warming up. There's a closed-circuit TV showing what's happening out in the hall, but it doesn't do any of the voices justice. I watch for two minutes before deciding that it's crap.

I'm going backstage.

And like I thought, there's no comparison. Just a few feet away from me, a tenor from Texas is singing to a packed house. Onstage where he is, it feels like hundreds of people are right on top of you. Here in the wings, though, it's just me and the stage manager.

Then I see a movement to my left.

Kathryn is standing under an acoustic panel nearby. I nod at her. She nods back, and we watch while the tenor finishes his pieces. He sweeps past us off the stage as the next competitor goes on. We watch her perform, too—a mezzo with a bad case of the shakes. "Yikes," Kathryn says when the girl hits a sour note.

"Yeah," I say. And I don't know why, but a question comes into my head—one I've been wanting to ask for a long time. It has nothing to do with the Blackmore. There's no reason to ask it now, except that Kathryn is standing here, and this might be my only chance.

"I just want to know one thing," I say.

"What?" She never looks away from the stage.

"Last year. Did you really just tell Chloe and Dina about my dad and Jake?"

"Yes."

"Did you tell anybody else?"

"No."

"Okay."

I believe her.

So who posted all those things online? Was it Chloe? Dina? A wannabe like Laura Lindner? Maybe it was somebody totally random—someone who saw Jake and my dad out together or worked on a movie set and wanted to impress people with some gossip. Whoever it was, it doesn't matter now. Life went on for Dad. Jake's a bigger star than ever. And what happened between me and Kathryn happened. We can't change it, even if we wanted to.

"Miss Dempsey?" A monitor taps me on the shoulder as the fifth person, a baritone, starts to sing. "You know you're next, right?"

"Right," I say. Behind him I can see Hildy at the stage door. I go to her for one last pep talk.

"Remember to let your breath do the work," she tells me. "Don't forget to acknowledge Joan when you bow. Loosen your shoulders. Oh! And these just arrived."

They are lilies—the same red ones that will be given to tonight's winner. I fish a card out of the green tissue paper.

To my Little Star!
Best of luck, Daddy

I fold the card and put it back.

"Should I put them in your dressing room?" Hildy asks.

I nod. The monitor clears his throat. "Miss Dempsey? We're ready."

"Okay." I turn back toward the stage, but then stop.

Reaching up to my neck, I unfasten the silver pendant.

"Take this, too," I say. Hildy holds out her hand, and I set the necklace on her palm. I see the little star sparkle before she closes her fingers around it. I can do this without my dad. I know that now. It's not reassuring, or healing, or even all that sad. It's just the truth. I can do it without him because I have to.

The stage is empty. I put my hand to my throat and feel nothing there but my own skin. Nothing but me.

"Good luck," says Kathryn as I walk past her.

"You too," I say.

Then I step out onto the stage.

KATHRYN

THERE IS SOMETHING ABOUT A moment like this, the breath just before a decision is announced, that makes every possibility real. In that moment, all options are open; you can choose whichever one you want, and it is yours.

Until you're told that it isn't.

That is where we stand now: ten singers from around the U.S., each one waiting for the possibilities to narrow until time starts moving forward again.

Brooke stands at one end of the stage and I stand at the other. An old man steps out, followed by three college girls carrying bouquets. He holds five checks in his hand, each of which is folded into a business-sized envelope. I focus on the checks, thinking about the diamond-filled casket in "The Jewel Song" that tempts a young girl into envisioning an easier, more glamorous life.

I don't want glamour, I don't want riches. All I want is help, and the man now addressing the audience holds enough in his hands to ease my troubles, if not erase them altogether.

He talks about the new recital hall, about the fiftieth anniversary, about maddening, meaningless things so that I start to tune him out. And then, cruelly quick, he starts to announce the winners.

Fifth place goes to a baritone from Kentucky. Fourth to a soprano from Oregon. I pray not to hear my own name, but in doing so I fear I've harnessed a possibility—one I didn't want.

"Third place: From Lake Champion, Minnesota—Miss Kathryn Pease."

A bouquet is thrust into my arms, along with an envelope. I look down to see *$5,000* written across it in blue ballpoint ink just as I hear my father shout from the audience, "Brava!"

Tears of disappointment spring into my eyes and my face burns with the sting of failure. I'm surprised, though, to find another emotion underneath: relief, and beyond that, something I never expected—a whole new set of possibilities stretching out before me. There will be no box of jewels, no twenty-five-thousand-dollar check to make it all easier; I will have to explore each possibility myself, then make happen the ones that I choose instead of waiting for someone—or something— to do it for me.

Cradling my flowers, I hold back the tears and look for Brooke. She stands at the end of the row with her eyes closed, and for the first time since I've known her I see fear on her face. A different energy emanates from her now: a want so raw that I am embarrassed to have noticed it.

Suddenly another possibility comes to me: What if Brooke doesn't place at all? What if my little win turns out to be a victory over her?

The second-place winner is announced; Brooke winces. A few months ago I would have enjoyed the idea of hurting her but now, with the prospect so close, I find no satisfaction in it. All I really wanted was the money, and if I can't have that, then I don't care who wins.

Actually, that's not true; in this moment, I care very much.

I find myself sending out an energy of my own, focusing on the last envelope in the old man's hand as if I can affect what is written there. There are six singers left—six possibilities remaining. If prayer can pluck out one and crystallize it, then I am determined to make that happen.

"First place: The winner of the Fiftieth Annual Black-more Young Artists' Festival . . ."

Let it be . . . , I think, concentrating with everything I have. *Let it be her.* . . .

" . . . Miss Brooke Lynne Dempsey."

Brooke opens her eyes slowly, nodding as if to absorb the weight of what this means, as the giant first-place bouquet is placed in her arms. I join the applause, but not before wiping tears from my cheeks.

I watch as, arms filled with lilies, Brooke begins to make her way along the line of other competitors. She truly is beautiful, in a way that high school guys could never appreciate; but someday, somebody will see her for what she really is—an incredible and incredibly talented girl—and then she'll never go dateless again.

When she reaches me, she stops. I raise my arms because I'm not sure what else to do, and she leans in for the hug.

"Hey," she says into my ear. "I'm sorry."

"No, I'm really happy for you." I let her go and try to show with my eyes that I really mean it. "You deserve this."

One of the college students comes over and puts her arm behind Brooke, trying to nudge her faster down the line and toward a group of important-looking people waiting in the wings.

"I don't know what we're doing after this," she tells me, trying to hang back. "Maybe dinner at the coffee shop. I'm starving. See you there?"

"Sure," I say, and then she's moved on. As I watch her turn and bow to the audience, I know that the long story isn't about the two of us anymore.

That story is over. It's time to start a new one—a story all my own.

ACKNOWLEDGMENTS

It's amazing how many people it takes to see one little book to publication. I am eternally grateful to:

My agent, Holly Root, for believing in me and refusing to give up.

My editor, Erica Sussman, for taking my story under her wing and giving it the chance to succeed. Her spot-on revision notes didn't hurt, either!

All of my awesome friends, both online and in real life, including my buddies at LiveJournal, the members of the teenlitauthors group, The Tenners, The Elevensies, and my fellow debuts at 2K11.

The many, many talented writers who read *Rival* and helped make it better. I was honored to get feedback and encouragement from Sara Zarr, Lauren Barnholdt, Mandy Hubbard, L. K. Madigan, April Henry, Melodye Shore, Lisa Donnelly, Dorothy Crane Imm, and DeAnn

Marie O'Toole. Special thanks to Mary Pleiss and Darcy Vance, who really "got" this story and gave it a little extra love along the way.

Jody Feldman, for giving my music competition a prettier name.

Teresa Buchholz and James Bagwell, for helping me get the music references just right.

My dad, who always made me feel taken care of, my mom the English teacher, who had me reading Shakespeare and watching *Masterpiece Theatre* in grade school, and my sister, who dragged me away from the computer once a month to go "fashion bashin'" at the ballet.

Most important, thank you, thank you, thank you to my wonderful husband, who gave me the time, space, and support to write, and who never once referred to my book as "a hobby." I love you with all my heart.